SOLDIER

BATTLE OF THE BULGE

DOGS

READ ALL THE

SOLDIER DOGS

BOOKS!

SOLDIER
BATTLE OF THE BULGE
DOGS

MARCUS SUTTER

ILLUSTRATIONS BY ANDIE TONG

HARPER FESTIVAL

An Imprint of HarperCollinsPublishers

HarperFestival is an imprint of HarperCollins Publishers.

Soldier Dogs #5: Battle of the Bulge
Text copyright © 2019 by HarperCollins Publishers
Illustrations copyright © 2019 by Andie Tong
www.harpercollinschildrens.com
ISBN 978-0-06-295794-8
Typography by Rick Farley
19 20 21 22 23   PC/LSCH   10 9 8 7 6 5 4 3 2 1
❖
First Edition

This book is dedicated to all the brave soldiers—whether they walked on two legs or four—who drove the Nazis out of Belgium. We remember.

PROLOGUE

The air in the Ardennes forest was thick with silence.

Guns fired. Tanks rumbled. Men called to each other through the trees. The sounds of war echoed around them, and yet somehow the vast, dense sprawl of the Ardennes swallowed them all up. The only sounds Juliette could hear were the ice cracking beneath her and her own heartbeat.

She stood on the surface of the frozen river, halfway across, staring down at a German soldier.

★ 1 ★

His scarf and goggles obscured his face. Between that and his long black coat, he looked like a drawing from a storybook she'd once read, about the Grim Reaper playing chess with an ordinary man.

The dogs they'd traveled with, Boss and Delta, were crouched and ready to strike at the soldier, but they couldn't help her.

Juliette shifted her right foot an inch.

Beneath her came the muffled crack of splitting ice.

Throughout the Ardennes, buried in the freezing hills and thick pines, two sides were waging a dire war. Hungry, tired, and far from home, the Allied and German troops both sought a victory that would decide the fate of the world. If the Germans pushed into the enemy front, they would finally overwhelm the American military and stop their advance farther into Belgium. It would deal a blow that might force the US troops to slowly lose the ground they'd gained since invading France earlier in the year. If the Americans won, they could drive the occupying Germans farther and farther north, take back the port of Antwerp, liberate Belgium, and deal Hitler a humiliating blow. German morale would be destroyed. It might even lead to the end of the war.

Juliette wanted the Americans to win. She wanted her country back and the war to be over.

But right now, all that mattered was that the ice beneath them held.

"What do we do?" whispered Antoine behind her. Juliette had never liked her neighbor, but right now he sounded as different as possible from the bully she knew. The fear in his voice echoed the tension hanging around them.

"I don't know," she admitted.

Beneath her, there was another soft rumble, and a new crack appeared in the ice at her feet.

"We need to run," said Antoine, giving in to total panic. "We've got to—"

"No!"

Before she could get the words out, Antoine was spinning to head back the way they'd just come. She could see the accident moments before it happened: his unsure footing, the fear in his stride, and the slippery snow on the ice beneath his feet.

Her heart seized. Antoine's foot went out from under him, and he fell to the frozen surface with a sickening thud.

Juliette heard the ice cracking beneath her. She felt a quick shock under her feet. Boss and Delta turned to her and whined, their ears able to pick up the barely audible sounds.

More silence.

Antoine looked up with half a smile and said, "I think we're okay."

"Whew," sighed Juliette.

There was another cracking nose, and the ice underneath her feet fell through.

CHAPTER 1

Juliette saw her chance. She'd have to move quickly.

She tossed her doll to Alix and sprinted across the courtyard. The cobblestones beneath her feet were uneven and cracked, but she'd walked them her whole life, and she could nimbly leap over any obstacle in her path.

The boys barely even saw her coming. They thought they could continue their soccer game uninterrupted. But they'd made a vital mistake— they'd passed to Luca Diget, a disorganized boy, who dribbled like he was trying to dance around the ball. The minute Juliette had seen it come his way, she knew she had an in.

She flew past Luca so quickly, he barely had time to yell, "Hey!" In an instant she had the ball, and she expertly dodged the boys who sprinted toward her. They all rushed her at once, yelling and carrying on.

She easily dribbled to the end of the courtyard and faced the goal—a section of brick wall between two trash cans. Antoine Marzen crouched there, hands out and brow set, a mean scowl beneath his stupid bowl cut. Juliette grinned and drank up Antoine's anger at the sight of her. She was going to enjoy this.

She faked—left, right, left—and came down hard with her right foot. Antoine darted to the right, anticipating her kick . . . but she held back at the last minute, and he landed in a pile of rotten cloth and old newspaper. As Antoine sputtered from the garbage at her feet, Juliette neatly kicked the ball against the wall, where it smacked the brick and rolled back to her!

"WHOO!" she yelled, and threw her fists into

the air. When she turned back to the other kids, she saw that no one else shared her excitement. The boys all crossed their arms and sneered at her. George Gurn, who had gotten the ball for Christmas a few days ago, picked it up and clutched it to his chest. Luca Diget's round cheeks were bright red with anger. In the background, Alix and the other girls stared at Juliette like she'd decided to chew rocks.

"See? I told you!" yelled Antoine, brushing a shred of damp smelling paper from his arm and pointing at her. "I told you it would be like this! We can't even have her *around*. She should be banned from this courtyard."

"You're just upset that you're a bad goalie," said Juliette.

A murmur of disbelief ran through the kids. If a boy had said such a thing, Juliette knew, it might mean a fight. Part of her hoped Antoine would try to fight her and give her an excuse to show him what for. He screwed up his face, looking like he was about to burst with rage—but at the last minute, he took a deep breath, brushed down his pants one last time, and then faced the boys with a calm regard.

"The war will never end if girls act like this," he said calmly.

The boys all nodded and rumbled in agreement.

Now it was Juliette's turn to feel angry. "Shut up," she said.

"My father says that the only way for us to come out of the war alive is for everyone to do as they're supposed to," he announced. "Men should fight and work, and women should look after their families. That's how things are supposed to be."

Juliette felt a hot sting behind her cheeks as the other boys began nodding and murmuring along. She hated how good Antoine was at acting calm and serious instead of lashing out at her. He was the sort of boy parents thought was sweet and clever, when really he just never got loud when he wanted to be mean. He reminded her of the Nazi soldiers who had occupied Belgium, so good at sounding thoughtful when they just wanted their way.

She looked to Alix and the other girls for support, but they all had their heads bowed. None of them wanted to speak up and be one of the troublesome people Antoine was talking about.

"That's not true!" she cried out. "Plenty of women have fought in the war! There's that spy in France, Linda Martin!"

Antoine remained unfazed. "If you ask me, we should kick Juliette out of this courtyard. She's not allowed to play with us anymore."

"Yeah!" shouted Luca Diget. "Banish her!"

The other boys began agreeing, crying "Banish her!" and "Get her out of here!" Juliette's heart beat fast as she listened to all of them yelling, telling her to leave. And all the while Antoine smiled at her like he'd won some immense victory. Even the boys she liked talking to, Theo and Milos, began to nod along, sucked into Antoine's act. She felt as if she were boiling inside as she stared at his stupid little smirk . . . and suddenly her anger overflowed.

"Shut *UP!*" she yelled, and before even thinking about it, she shoved Antoine hard. He sprawled backward and fell to the cobblestones with a thud. Everyone went silent, and two of the other boys ran to help Antoine up.

"See," he grumbled as he stood. "This is *exactly* what I'm talking about."

Juliette blinked hard. She felt tears, hot and heavy, swelling behind her eyes. But the last thing she wanted to do was let Antoine see her cry, so she turned and ran, letting the tears be swept back across her face as she went, flying back home as quickly as she could.

As she ran down onto Rue l'glise and into the center of Plainevaux, she caught a glimpse of the red Nazi flag hanging on the side of one building. Today, the sight of it reminded her of a secret she held. Something that Antoine would never know about or understand.

The thought put a spring in her step as she headed down the street toward her parents' bakery. It used to be that you could smell Privot family bread all over town. These days, with supplies so thin, a few loaves and scones were often the best they could do.

But we still have enough to share, she thought, and smiled again at her own little secret.

She was so distracted that she didn't notice the scene going on inside the bakery until she'd barreled through the door and skidded to a halt.

At the front counter stood Papa, his big, brave eyes lined with fear as he glared down at her. Across from him stood a man in a long, black-leather coat and a military uniform beneath it.

The customer stared at her with dead eyes, and then his lips curled back into a smile that terrified Juliette.

"Good afternoon, fräulein," said the man in black in accented French. *"Heil Hitler."*

CHAPTER 2

TWO RIVERS, ALASKA
DECEMBER 29, 1944
12:20 A.M. LOCAL TIME

Gregor whistled, and Boss felt her energy instantly spike. She was already pretty tired—they all were—but they were also trained to follow Gregor's orders. And when he whistled, no matter how tired they were, they came running.

She bounded through the snow alongside her pack, relishing the feeling of the cold white flakes billowing around her. She moved in long, loping strides, and she felt how her body was made to move through the deep snow. It felt good to be out here, doing what she was trained to do.

That said, she was definitely getting tired.

Boss glanced at Buzz, her closest packmate, and saw that she was lagging too, her tongue lolling out and her bright eyes glancing around, asking the same question she was asking inside: Why the long hike? Why was Gregor taking them so far out for so long? Usually at this time of day they were just getting up, eating a bowl of morning chow, and going for their first patrol around the base. But they'd been awake for hours, and they had wandered miles from the fence. Something was up.

Tank, their alpha, acted as though he couldn't care less. That picked up Boss's spirits as much as Gregor's whistle—seeing Tank being strong for them, leading them with honor and energy. She also noticed Delta doing her best to cover up her heavy breathing and tired eyes, and she told herself that she had to rally, to push forward, if only so that Delta didn't show her up.

They all bounded up to Gregor, who smiled from beneath his icy lip-fur and held up his hand, which was his signal to stop and sit and wait.

When the whole pack was seated at his feet, he walked down the line and one by one gave them an ear scratch or a face pat, and said their names in that deep, reassuring voice of his.

"Boss," he said when he stroked the side of her face. She tilted her head and pressed it into his palm, and Gregor laughed the way he always did when she responded to him. She liked Gregor; he was better than the human master they'd had before, the tall, loud man who barked commands and ordered the pack into separate kennels every night.

Gregor whistled again and waved them up the snowy rise of a mountain ridge, and the pack followed him. Even before they got to the ridge, Boss knew what he was going to show them. It was the thing they couldn't smell, the great big thing that seemed to always paralyze him.

They crested the hill and stared out over a snow-filled valley between the mountains. Overhead, in the sky, there shimmered two lines of light that swayed and faded in and out of each other in the sky. Boss watched them in awe, still not quite understanding them. They had no smell, made no sound, and yet they danced in the air above them, like two angry dogs made of light fighting each other.

"Look," said Gregor, and pointed to them. He said the words humans always used for the dogs in the sky—"Northern Lights!" Boss heard Gregor's heartbeat speed up as she stared at the sky.

She was happy the lights pleased Gregor. He was a good human, a fair master. She knew he was going to put them in danger eventually. She wasn't a dumb dog—she understood what the training was for. But she appreciated that he was good to them while he did it, and that something in his world made him feel like his master had said, "Good boy, Gregor. Good boy."

She felt it building, first in her heart and then moving up her throat. She could tell the rest of the pack was feeling it too—the love for Gregor, the wonder at the lights in the sky, the power of the woods all around them. It built and rose until . . .

Boss was the first: she leaned her head back and howled, high and loud, into the air. One by

one, the other members of the pack followed, and Gregor, all smiles, joined them.

When they were done, Gregor whistled again, and they began running back down the hill to base. The slope gave Gregor and the pack a little speed, and soon Boss was leaping through huge mounds of snow, her tongue dangling from the side of her open mouth as she launched herself down the mountain alongside Tank and the pack.

As they got near the bottom of the mountain, new smells filled the air, and Boss shared a glance with Buzz. They weren't unfamiliar smells necessarily, just uncommon—burning chemicals, greasy rubber, sweating humans. The sounds were also familiar, but louder and quicker than usual.

They made their way through a patch of woods and broke through the tree line.

Boss's ears perked.

The plane was being prepared. The bay door was open, and men ran in and out, loading boxes, packs . . . and even the sled, which was being taken off the back of a truck.

Gregor whistled and lead the pack forward, through the fence, over to the plane. Suddenly, Boss was standing in formation, left of Buzz, behind Tank, part of two rows of dogs waiting at the ramp leading onto the plane.

Boss couldn't help but whine. Just like that, they were on the mission. Just like that, it was war.

CHAPTER 3

Juliette felt frozen to the spot. The Nazi officer stared down at her, his bright, intense eyes sunk deep in bruise-colored sockets. His black coat and the black hat with a silver skull at its center made his face seem to float, white and ghastly, in a great sweep of shadow.

"Your daughter?" asked the officer, not looking back at Papa.

Papa's mustache twitched for a moment, and then he sighed and said, "Yes."

The Nazi waited and looked annoyed. "Does

she have a name, Herr Privot?"

"Juliette," Papa said softly.

"Very pretty," said the officer. "Hello, Juliette. I am General Esser. A pleasure to meet you, young lady. This is my associate, Private Gerhardt."

Juliette whirled at the sound of shuffling. Another Nazi stood in a corner, this one younger, in an infantry uniform and sloping metal helmet. Juliette immediately noticed that he looked unwell—his cheeks were waxy and pale, and he breathed slowly and steadily. His uniform looked too large for him and hung from his body.

The excitement Juliette had felt turned to icy dread. Pinpricks of cold crept along the back of her scalp, and her breath hitched.

Nazis. Two of them, in her family's bakery. After weeks of not being bothered.

They know, thought Juliette.

"Juliette," Papa said roughly, "manners."

She curtsied and mumbled, "Good afternoon, General."

"Juliette, perhaps you can help me," said General Esser, sweeping a gloved hand around her and ushering her up to the counter. Juliette had an image of herself being led to the gallows, and shuddered. "You see, your father does not seem to understand how grave his situation is."

"I've given you all the bread I can spare," said Papa, trying to sound strong. "You have your rations, and I have your government's promise that my bakery will not be—"

"I tell him that war is coming to your town," said the Nazi. "That there are American soldiers out in the woods around him, and that soon his city will be swarming with angry, tired German soldiers who will want bread and not care much about the law. I offer to protect him from them for a few extra loaves of bread. And he says no. He says, *I do not want your help.* It is . . . frustrating. So I was thinking perhaps you could ask him for me. Will you try?"

General Esser got down on one knee next to Juliette. She couldn't see his face so much as feel it, cold and pale, next to hers.

"Say to him, *Please, Papa,*" he said, making his voice high and plaintive. "*Please, for my sake . . . give the general his bread.*"

Juliette locked eyes with Papa. She could tell

that her father, the broad-shouldered and tidy man she'd always thought of as stronger than anything, was frightened. For himself, for her, for their whole family . . . and for something else. Juliette knew he shared the same terror she did . . . and the hope that came with it.

If they wanted the bread, they did not know. If they did not know, then all was not lost.

Juliette nodded. Papa blinked but did not move.

"You may have the last loaves in the front window." Papa sighed. "I will not have any more before morning."

"Much obliged, Herr Privot," said the general. He rose and slapped his thigh, and in an instant the infantryman was at the display shelves up front with his rucksack open, jamming in the remaining loaves of *Graubrot*—the dense, dark rye bread the Germans insisted Papa make for soldiers. When he got to the last one, he couldn't help himself, and he took a furious bite of it, chewing with his stuffed mouth open. The general clucked at him, and the Nazi soldier reluctantly shoved the loaf in his bag with the others.

"We are eternally grateful, sir," said General Esser, tipping his hat. "When our compatriots come to town, we will tell them you are off-limits. In the meantime, if you see any Americans, let me know . . . I'll be around again, I'm sure."

CHAPTER 4

The Nazis blew out the door and down the street with a clicking of boot heels. Papa waited for a full thirty seconds before he rushed over and swept Juliette into his arms.

"I'm sorry, Papa," she said between quick, worried breaths. "If I'd seen them . . ."

"It doesn't matter," he said, "as long as you're all right." He pulled her out at arm's length and gave her that big, heart-warming smile of his . . . and then, slowly, it faded away to a frown. Juliette knew that face—it was time to work. Without another word, the two walked behind the counter, past the old curtain, and into the kitchen.

The minute they got into the back, Mama launched out of the stairwell leading up to their small apartment, her face drawn and worried. When she saw Juliette she ran over, seized her face, and looked her over.

"Are you all right?" she asked. "Where have you been?"

"Playing with the other children," she said softly. "I didn't see the Germans in here until it was too late."

"It's all right." Mama sighed and then immediately turned to Papa. "What did they want?"

"More bread," said Papa, busily walking to his desk in the one corner of the dusty back room. "They've eaten all their rations, and used all their tickets, and now they want it for free."

Juliette sneered at the very thought. The Nazis were bullies, just like Antoine. When the Germans had occupied and taken over Belgium, everyone had been assured that they would be fair and orderly. They were issued their own rations, and occasionally they got tickets to spend at local shops. But soon they stopped listening to opinions and started barking orders. They demanded bakers make the military ration bread, *Graubrot*. Plainevaux didn't have that many soldiers stationed here, so her Papa had been able to stay afloat. But now it sounded like the war was on its way, and with all the supply routes around them cut off, the Nazis were somehow becoming even meaner.

That's what was wrong with the infantryman, she realized—hunger. It was why he'd eaten that big bite of bread, even with his commanding officer watching. The soldiers must be starving.

No time to worry about that now, she thought. More important things to do.

"Do they know?" said Mama.

"No," said Papa.

"Oh, thank goodness." Mama moaned and crossed herself.

"But he said that the war is finally coming here," Papa said quickly. "American soldiers are invading the Ardennes, and the Germans are on their way to counter them."

Mama's relief vanished.

"We need to leave," she said.

"Yes," said Papa with a nod. "Tonight. Take your time in case they're still in the area and it looks like we're rushing, but start packing. We'll head to Lierneux. I've been told there's a spot open there. We'll go tonight."

Juliette blinked, not understanding. "But . . . we need to go warn them," she said, pointing out their small back window, to the woods and the secret within them.

Papa swallowed and shook his head. "It's too dangerous right now. The general may be watching us. I'm sorry, Juliette."

"But," said Juliette, "but Masha—"

"That is *final*," boomed Papa, though Juliette heard the crack in his voice. "Get your things. Only what you can carry. We leave in an hour and a half."

Juliette trudged up the stairs to her family's flat, feeling numb.

They were just going to leave them out there.

She stormed through their tiny apartment, ignoring the fireplace and table, the garlands of green holly on the mantels left over from

Christmas, looking pale and sickly. She went straight to her room and dug the cloth-wrapped package out from under her mattress. Inside the wrappings sat a small knife and a hunk of wood that, if you squinted at it right, looked like a little girl.

Juliette stared at the carving and let the cold wash over her.

Somewhere inside her, flint struck.

No.

She wrapped the package and crammed it in the pocket of her coat. She ran to the kitchen, grabbed their last hunk of bread from the sideboard, and shoved it in the other pocket.

If there was one thing she could be, she knew, it was fast. She could run for the back door and be out before her parents even saw her.

And if she ran quickly enough, she could get to her family's secret before the Germans did.

CHAPTER 5

A foot of snow lay in the woods outside of town, and though Juliette was nimble on the cobblestone street, she couldn't exactly race through the knee-high layer over everything. On top of that, she forced herself to walk in zigzags, like Papa had taught her, so as to not leave obvious tracks in the snow. Now, deep in the Ardennes forest with the night closed in around her, her feet were close to going numb, and try as she might to hug warmth into herself, a chill found its way down her neck.

She should've thought this out better. She should turn back. She—

No.

Juliette put her head down, set her jaw, and kept trudging through the snow.

She had to warn them. And she had to do it fast.

If there was one thing she'd learned since the war started, it was that everything could change in an instant.

She'd been only seven when Germany had occupied Belgium and their lives had changed. She'd grown up loving her small town, enjoying school, helping out at the bakery, and playing with Alix and the other kids down the block. Things hadn't always been perfect—she'd fought with Antoine, and there were months when the bakery wasn't making as much money as it needed to—but they had been nice.

And then, just like that, Belgium had fallen. Nazi soldiers stormed in and started dragging the Privots' Jewish neighbors out of their homes and shoving them into the backs of trucks. Papa had told her about the ghettos, miserable towns built to house Jews . . . and then one day he'd refused to talk any further, as though seeing so many of his friends taken from their homes had cast a shadow over Papa. Suddenly, all he wanted to do was survive. He did what the soldiers asked, he made their *Graubrot* . . . whatever it took to protect his family.

Until that one night a few weeks before, when he'd come blustering up to their flat, taken Juliette and Mama by the fire, and whispered a secret to them.

There, up ahead. She could just spy the roof between the branches.

The cabin had belonged, Papa told her, to an old hunter who had let Papa rent it once when he was a boy. It certainly wasn't a very nice place— old, wooden, covered in patches of moss and clinging with dead ivy—but it was a fine spot to hole up in if you were looking to hunt rabbits.

Or avoid the Germans.

He'd found the family in the alley behind the bakery one night, eating scraps out of the garbage. Dirty, starving, exhausted, and terrified. A couple and their two children, a boy and a little girl.

They said their names were Kraisman. They said they'd come from Antwerp, one of Belgium's biggest cities, and that the Nazis were looking for them.

Papa knew harboring them was dangerous . . . but it was December. Christmastime, a season all about honoring a family lost in the wilderness.

He had remembered the cabin. So he'd taken them there.

Juliette couldn't stop herself—she jogged the last hundred feet, crashing through the snow, excited to show them what she'd been working on and to warn them that they were no longer safe in—

Juliette froze.

The cabin door was open.

CHAPTER 6

N oise everywhere. Wind on all sides. No smells. No smells? That couldn't be right.

Boss raised her head and blinked awake. She lay curled in one of the uncomfortable bucket seats within the plane, a web of seat belts holding her down. Her vision blurred, and she had to shake her head and give a preliminary *Rrf* or two before she could really tell what was going on.

The whole pack was strapped into their bucket seats. The sled sat between them, huge and heavy, loaded with crates and supplies. Outside, propellers blazed with the most awful noise she'd ever heard. She could see light between the cracks around the door, but it was dim—they were definitely still in the evening, wherever they were.

Boss shook her head and tried to think. She couldn't believe this was actually happening. She couldn't . . .

Boss yawned hard. Why was she so sleepy? She realized she was wheezing, her tongue hanging out. There was something going on in the air. She could never really get her fill, no matter how fast she breathed. Was she sick?

"Boss." A hand touched her ear, and she looked up to see Gregor looking down at her. He gave her a big smile and shushed her, somehow knowing what she was feeling. He cooed more human things, but then said two words she understood: *down* and *parachute*.

The hum of the plane deepened, and Boss felt her stomach go weird. Bit by bit, the air got better, and she could breathe again. She let out a relieved bark, and noticed that one by one the other members of the pack opened their eyes and raised their heads.

The plane flew on for a few minutes before the human up front called back to Gregor, and Gregor walked down the aisle unsnapping their seat belts and letting them move around. When he released Boss, she jumped down onto the floor of the plane, shook off, and stood at attention, doing her best to ignore the roaring propeller and the cold floor beneath her paws.

Gregor walked down the length of the plane, making sure their harnesses were on tight. At the end of each check, he gave the dogs a clap on the back, to let them know it was go time. When his hand hit Boss, she felt an instant surge of energy run through her. This was it. There was no more training, no more hiking. Just the mission.

Gregor made his way to the front of the pack, finishing with Tank and Tank's partner, Dash. He gave the two lead dogs a clap on their backs, went to the door in the side of the plane . . . and yanked it open.

Suddenly, the inside of the plane rushed with noise and wind. The snow outside blasted the dying sunlight painfully back at them. A couple of her packmates barked and stepped back from the sudden hurricane of noise, light, and smells.

Gregor whistled, and Boss stood at attention. Out of the corner of her eye, she caught Delta doing the same, and hoped she was standing straighter and looking meaner than the other dog.

"Ready?" shouted Gregor, just like in training.

The pack lined up single file. Boss danced back and forth on her feet. She couldn't believe this. They were about to jump, in real life. "And . . . GO, GO, GO!" shouted Gregor. Tank ran up, Gregor grabbed him by the waist, and *WHOOSH*—he was gone out the window. The other dogs followed, one by one getting tossed into the open air by Gregor. When it was Boss's turn, she lowered her head, leapt, felt the tug as Gregor pulled her cord, and—

WHOOSH!

CHAPTER 7

Juliette crept slowly forward, trying to peer into the darkness beyond the door. She did her best to focus her hearing but could only make out the soft shushing of the swaying branches, the occasional plop of snow falling off a tree.

"Hello?" she said, feeling even smaller and more scared as she heard how tiny her voice sounded in the huge forest.

Her heart pounding, Juliette crept up to the door, peeked in, and saw . . .

Nothing.

"Hello?" she tried again, a little louder. She walked into the house and surveyed the scene. The front room stood dark and heavy with shadows, the huge overstuffed armchair looking like a coffin in silhouette. She had to be careful—for all she knew, there could be Nazi soldiers hiding in every corner—but she got the feeling she was all right. Something in her gut told her that there was no one else in the cabin.

Her heart pounded. Was she too late? Had the Nazis gotten here first?

She ran from room to room. The place had been left in a hurry, with blankets ripped off the bed. She kept hoping to walk in on them, to find the little girl, Masha, staring up at her with her big, dark eyes . . . but no. The house was empty as a tomb.

Her foot knocked against something on the floor, and she picked it up. It was a kind of wooden candelabra, painted gold. Papa had told her about this, about the holiday Jewish people celebrated instead of Christmas—Hanukkah, the festival of light. They lit candles on the candelabra, one every day for eight days. Masha said it was called a menorah.

Her heart weighed heavy as she turned it over in her hands. If they'd forgotten this, they must've left quickly. She placed the menorah gently on the ground. How long had they been gone? She hadn't seen any tracks.

Carefully, Juliette pulled the bundle from her one pocket and laid it out. The doll she was carving for Masha smiled up at her, only now its smile felt unfair, and cruel. Juliette felt sick that she'd never be able to give it to—

Boots in the snow.

Juliette jerked her head. Had she imagined it, or—

There. Again. And a cough.

Someone was coming. And by the sounds of it, they were right outside the door.

Juliette panicked. She spun around the room, looking for something to help her, somewhere to go or to hide. Her eyes locked on the dark space under the bed, and without thinking she grabbed the menorah and her doll and rolled underneath. Dust and cobwebs blew up into her face. They made her eyes itch and her nose feel funny, but she managed not to sputter.

The door opened, and heavy boots wandered into the front room. They paused . . . and then made their way slowly and carefully into the bedroom.

Juliette glanced out from under the bed. The black leather boots were dripping with icy snow and had hiking trousers tucked into them—whoever they belonged to, it was certainly not Mr. Kraisman. They walked slowly over to the edge of the bed and stopped, so close that Juliette could feel the cold from outside still radiating off of them.

Juliette felt her heart pounding in her ears. The intruder was right on top of her. She breathed quickly, trying to keep silent.

Dust tickled her nose, and before she could stop herself, she sneezed.

The boots jumped a little, and Juliette heard a gasp. Panic gripped her. She had to get out of here, *now*, to warn Mama and Papa. She wouldn't let the Nazis take her, like they'd taken their neighbors.

She'd go out fighting.

CHAPTER 8

Juliette grabbed her whittling knife. With a cry, she jabbed it out from under the bed, poking a hole in the trousers above the boot. The intruder screamed, stumbled back, and fell to the ground with a thud. Instantly, Juliette leapt out from under the bed, brandishing her whittling knife at . . .

Antoine, who glowered up at her from the floor, clutching the side of his leg, his eyes wet with tears.

The two neighbors froze for a moment,

breathing heavily and staring at each other with hurt, confused looks. As always, it was Antoine who made a fuss first, leaping to his feet and glaring at Juliette.

"What are you doing here?" he whispered.

"I—I was . . ." Juliette paused. Could she trust him? She wasn't sure—Antoine's father was a respected lawyer in town, one who sometimes befriended high-ranking members of the German government to gain his family favor. And Antoine . . . well, he was just a rude idiot who thought girls were meant to stay in the kitchen all day. But was he really a bad person, deep down?

She noticed the basket at his feet.

"What are all those?" she said, kneeling down to go through the contents.

"Leave that alone!" Antoine chided, but it was too late.

"Blankets?" she said, looking through the wicker basket. "Scarves?"

Juliette looked up at Antoine and saw the fear in his eyes—the same stark fear she'd felt earlier, when she'd walked into her family's bakery and found the Nazis waiting for her. She reached into her other pocket and removed the last loaf of *Graubrot* to show Antoine. His shoulders fell and a long, relieved breath escaped him.

"How long have you been helping them?" she asked.

"I found them here two weeks ago, while I was out on a hike," said Antoine softly. "They were freezing in the snow, and I thought . . ." He looked away, sniffed loudly, and wiped his nose with the sleeve of his coat. "What about you?"

Juliette put the bread back in her pocket and told him about her Papa helping the Kraismans for the last few weeks. She felt a great relief come over her as she finally said the story out loud. It had been such a burden, holding onto a secret that could get so many people taken away or worse. The confession felt as though she'd been keeping a hundred sparrows locked in her chest, and she'd finally opened the cage door.

"Do you have any idea where they've gone?" asked Antoine, glancing around the house. "I was here three days ago, and they were all bundled up inside." He glanced over his shoulder at her. "I always wondered where they'd gotten their food."

"They left something," she said. She stooped and grabbed her bundle and the menorah. "See? It's what they use to light candles for Hanukkah. I think they must have left in a hurry."

"It's just as well," said Antoine, peering around the front room, looking for clues. "The war's coming this way. Word is there are Americans dropping into France. It's got the Germans all frightened, and they've begun heading to this area."

"Two of them came to our bakery today," said Juliette. "I thought you might be one of them when you came in here . . . that's why I—" She raised the whittling knife feebly, suddenly feeling silly for charging out from under the bed ready to go to war with no one but her stupid neighbor.

Antoine touched the hole in his pants and rubbed his leg. "Good thing it was only a scratch. You're not strong enough to actually cut me."

Juliette felt her cheeks burn at the comment. Why did everything have to be an insult with him? "You seemed pretty upset when it happened."

"I was only startled," he said, sneering at her with his big, flat face. "What is that, anyway? Girls don't whittle."

"I was making something for Masha, the little Kraisman girl," she said, holding up her bundle.

She knew it was a mistake the minute she did it. In an instant, Antoine had snatched the doll away from her and was shoving her back as she scrambled to grab it. The boy lifted it high above his head, out of her reach, and she cursed herself for being smaller and weaker than he was.

"Shoddy craftsmanship," commented Antoine, examining the doll.

"Give that back!" yelled Juliette, clawing at his arm. "You have no right to take my things!" She lunged forward and grabbed ahold of it, and Antoine grunted as he wrestled it back and forth from her.

"Give it back!"

"Let it go!"

"I said—"

"They're in here!"

They both froze, their eyes going instantly wide. The last words had come from outside the cabin.

CHAPTER 9

Boss felt the wind in her ears—and her face, and tail, and every hair on her body. From above, the parachute went taut, and with a sharp tug she was no longer falling but floating gently through the air.

She barked with excitement, but also confusion. It was just night, and in the overcast grey sky she could barely make out the mountain ridges in the distance. Beneath her, the parachutes of her packmates floated down in a line like pads on a paw—but soon they were swallowed by the

shadows of trees beneath them. Where *were* they?

Boss breathed deep, savoring the cold air and the millions of smells coming to her as she descended. She wondered if any dog was as lucky as she was.

She tried to think critically, like a soldier, and survey her surroundings. There were a handful of white clearings around them, which would be good landing spots but bad for visibility. Otherwise, it was just dense forests, with trees so close together that she couldn't see the snowy ground between their branches. The goal would be to land, get harnessed to the sled, and get into the trees as quickly as possible so as to avoid being seen by the enemy.

The enemy. Boss glanced around her and realized how visible she and her packmates were. The enemy could probably see them from miles away . . . and if not them, the sled.

She looked over her shoulder and saw the sled above them, dropping with the help of two parachutes. She worried that it might break on impact . . . but then she saw Gregor above it. Saw the determined look on his face. The sight bucked up Boss's spirits. They'd be all right, so long as he was looking out for them.

She heard a bark from below, and saw that Tank and Dash had landed in the nearest clearing. Boss lowered her ears and raised her feet. Time to do what she was trained for.

CHAPTER 10

Juliette and Antoine had just crouched down behind the overstuffed armchair when the door flew open with a bang. They huddled together, their backs pressed against the chair, trying to make themselves as flat and small as possible.

Carefully, they craned their necks back and peeked around the edge of the chair.

Two German soldiers, guns raised, stomped slowly into the front room, shaking snow from their boots. Silhouetted by the moonlight from outside, their long coats and sloped helmets made them look like phantoms.

"Show yourselves," bellowed the one in front in accented French, strafing a flashlight around the room.

Juliette wondered if the soldiers could hear her heart beating. It was certainly pounding fast enough.

After a moment of silence, the second German strode into the house. He did a lap of the rooms, making a racket as he threw open cupboards and drawers, his flashlight throwing weird shadows around the cabin. He finally stormed back into the front room, grumbling, "Nothing. Not even a crust of bread." Then he strode toward them purposefully. He turned, and Juliette felt her fear spike as he flopped right into the armchair they crouched behind. The two spoke in German, and listening hard, Juliette could make out the basic words she'd learned at school and from Papa and Mama.

"See?" said the one in the chair. "You were hearing things."

"There were voices, Till," said the one still

standing. He closed the door and circled the room. When he got close, Juliette saw his face in a shaft of moonlight from the window and recognized him as Gerhardt, the soldier from the bakery that morning. "I'm sure of it."

"It's probably hunger," grumbled Till. "I've been hungry for weeks now."

Gerhardt said nothing but absentmindedly reached into his pocket and pulled out a brown block half wrapped in foil. He took a bite and chewed, though he made a face. He held it out to Till, but he shook his head.

"I thought you were hungry," said Gerhardt.

"I don't want another ration bar," said Till, and suddenly he began speaking quickly and angrily. "I want chocolate, and coffee, and good bread. I want a roll with a wurst in it, and maybe some noodles. Remember those, Gerhardt? I can almost taste them. Instead, we're stuck here, in these freezing woods, eating terrible rations, all for some stupid, miserable war. And now, thousands more of us are going to come here to fight the Americans. It's going to be a madhouse."

"Easy, Till," said Gerhardt. "Words like those

could get you punished . . . or worse."

"Gerhardt, why are we still fighting this horrible war?" ranted Till, sitting forward and holding his hands out to his countryman. "We're running out of supplies. The Americans and English are coming, but from what we've heard, they're also out of food. This forest is going to be a battleground for two starving armies for . . . for what? So that Hitler can have a Europe without Jews, or blacks, homosexuals, and everyone else he just decides to deem *inferior*? So that he can take over the entire world? I am sick of fighting and killing, Gerhardt. I just want to go home."

Juliette considered that information. Soldiers were coming . . . but they were running out of food. More important, she heard the strain in the Nazi soldier's voice, the sadness and panic behind his words. He was as sick of the war as any of the people in her town.

"We do it for the glory of Germany," said Gerhardt.

"*You* do it for the glory of Germany!" said Till, rising to his feet and storming toward

Gerhardt. "But I don't even know what that means, and I'm sick of—"

There was a skittering noise as Till's boot collided with something that slid across the floor. The Nazi soldiers' eyes followed it. Gerhardt bent down, picked it up, and held it up.

Juliette's heart leapt. She felt Antoine gasp behind her.

"What's that?" asked Till, peering at the gold-painted candleholder.

"It's a *menorah*," said Gerhardt, spitting the last word as though it tasted foul. "It's for Jewish black magic. They light candles in it and summon the devil."

"Nonsense," said Till, but glanced around the room nervously. "Really? I've heard stories, but never believed . . ."

"If this is here, this place is probably cursed," said Gerhardt. "More important, there have been Jews here. Let's head back to town and start knocking on doors. This cabin isn't so far out that none of these mountain hicks knows about it. Odds are, someone was harboring them, and I'd like to know who."

Gerhardt pulled a small flask, like a miniature canteen, from his belt. He unscrewed the cap and flung a clear liquid from it onto the floor. Juliette's nostrils burned as a chemical smell filled the air.

"Kerosene?" asked Till. "You're not planning to . . ."

"Let's clean the filth off this place," said Gerhardt.

He drew a box of matches from his coat, shook one out, and lifted his left boot to strike it on his heel. Juliette's stomach rose to her throat as she heard the sulfur head sizzle and pop.

The Nazi tossed the match casually to the floor. With a *FWUMPF*, the floor of the cabin burst into flames.

CHAPTER 11

OVER TOUL, FRANCE
DECEMBER 29, 1944
5:53 A.M. LOCAL TIME

As the snowy clearing came up to meet Boss, she started running in air, just like she'd practiced at the base. She hit the ground, ran a few yards out to let her parachute drag, and then used her mouth to unbuckle it.

There! Perfect dismount! She stood up straight, head held proudly to the sky, and took in her surroundings with excitement. No mountain would be too high for her! No river too deep! No—

THUD! Delta came swooping down too close

and slammed into her side, sending Boss sprawling. Both dogs got tangled in Delta's parachute.

Fury raged through Boss. Stupid Delta could never get things right. She was always messing up Boss's best chances to be a good soldier dog. Without thinking, Boss showed her teeth and let loose a low growl. Delta did the same, and suddenly they were twisting and snarling and biting at each other, getting further and further tangled in the net of parachute cords that tightened around them.

Then one bark drowned both of their voices out. Boss and Delta stopped their fighting and whined.

Tank looked down at them and growled low and steady in the back of his throat. Boss felt her heart break as she saw the look in his eyes—disappointment. Boss wanted to whine, to point out that she'd landed like a pro and it was Delta's fault, but it was obvious that Tank wanted none of it. She lowered her ears, bowed her head, and went quiet.

A moment later, Gregor touched down, and he helped Boss and Delta untangle from each other. There was a loud crash in the snow nearby, and Boss looked up to see the sled, its two extra-large parachutes draping slowly over it. Gregor whistled and waved the pack to his side.

All ten dogs stood in formation, with Tank and his neighbor Dash up front, Boss and Buzz directly behind them. Boss did everything in her power not to click her teeth at Delta as she trotted by. It would be a stupid move—there was nothing Gregor liked less than an angry or mean dog. There had been a handful of them in Boss's first obedience training class, dogs like Chief and Flare and Zigzag—always fighting, always showing their teeth. Gregor hadn't wasted time in sending them off to other packs or missions.

She wouldn't be that kind of dog. She'd be a good soldier. If Delta did something that made her look bad, she'd be even better. That was how good she was.

Gregor tied the dogs together and climbed onto the sled behind them. Boss looked to her side and locked eyes with her partner, Buzz. Buzz nodded, looking a little ruffled but ready to go. That was Buzz—ready for anything. That's why she and Buzz were swing dogs, stationed right behind Tank and Dash, trained to help steer the sled down the easiest path. Delta was just a team dog, one of the pullers.

Gregor whistled. His whip cracked.

Just like that, they were off.

CHAPTER 12

The Nazis stormed out of the house, leaving Antoine and Juliette alone in the burning cabin, doing their best to stifle their coughs as smoke filled the air. When the door closed behind them, Juliette rose to try and put out the fire—but Antoine yanked her back down.

"We're going to burn alive!" she cried, her eyes stinging as oily black smoke rose into them.

"They might still be out there," he whispered. "Get down. Here, follow me."

Juliette hadn't realized that Antoine had

grabbed his basket of blankets when they fled behind the chair. He pulled the bundle out and unrolled it across the flames between them and bedroom door, smothering them.

"Come on," he said, and crawled across the blanket. Juliette followed, feeling the searing heat on either side of her and coughing out smoke. By now, the flames had crept up the wooden walls of the cabin and were beginning to lick at the rafters. They didn't have a second to lose—if they didn't move now, the whole place was going to burn down on top of them.

Once they were in the bedroom, Antoine gently closed the door and pointed to the back window. "Crawl out of there," he said. "We'll escape out back."

Juliette cracked the window and crawled outside, landing with a grunt in the snow beneath. She worried the noise might attract the soldiers, but out here, all she could hear were crackling flames as the cabin's roof began to catch.

Antoine was half out the window when he pushed himself forward—and didn't budge. A startled, unbelieving look crossed his face.

"What's wrong?" asked Juliette.

"I'm stuck," he said.

"You're . . . oh no." Juliette looked into the window at Antoine's waist. One of his belt loops had caught on the inside sill, and he couldn't reach the snag.

"Hold still," she said, and wormed her thin little hands past him. Even through the growing smoke, she could see where Antoine's belt was caught on a nail. She grabbed her whittling knife, wormed it in, and begin cutting at the leather of his belt. She had to act fast—the air in the room had grown incredibly hot, and she could just make out the orange flicker of flames rising around the door.

Juliette squinted as she put her shoulders into it. She was almost . . . there . . .

SNAP! Antoine went flying out of the window and tumbling to the snow with a grunt. Juliette helped him stand and steadied him as he stumbled onto his feet. Together they both scurried into the woods.

The cabin was a wall of flames in no time. The two of them watched it at a distance as it lit up the forest, its light flickering between the trees, a column of thick smoke rising into the sky.

"Well, even if the Kraismans were out looking for food, they can't come back here now," grumbled Antoine, but Juliette's mind was elsewhere. She was thinking about the family, how they would feel if they came back to the cabin and found it gone. It was going to get so cold tonight, and she wondered if Masha had remembered her jacket. But even more than that, she thought about what the Nazis had said earlier. Thousands of them were about to overrun her town. There was no hiding from the war anymore. Her stomach sank, and she felt the backs of her eyes prickle.

She tried to swallow the lump in her throat and think this through. Mama and Papa had made it clear to her early on that there was always a possibility that the Germans would come to their door and take them away for no reason. "Nazis never need a reason," Mama had told her. They'd prepared her. If they were ever taken, or if it seemed like the war was finally bearing down on their town and they weren't around to help, she was supposed to tell Mrs. Burgo across the street that she wanted to "pick wildflowers," and Mrs. Burgo would hire someone to take her to . . .

"Lierneux," she said. "We have to head farther south, to Lierneux."

Antoine's eyes widened. "Are you out of your mind? We're not going there. If we walk, that's at least ten hours. We'd never get there before night-fall. Be rational."

Juliette's cheeks burned. How dare he speak to her like that? "Then we'll walk at night. Quit being a coward and come on."

"We need to wait for the American troops," said Antoine. "They're supposed to be here any day. My father says that if we can just hold out for a few more days—"

"You heard that soldier," said Juliette firmly. "They're going to start interrogating people around town. If that happens, I'm supposed to meet my parents in Lierneux. And if I don't meet them there, they might go looking for me. I can't risk that, not with our town being turned into a battlefield."

Antoine sighed and shook his head. "Listen to me," he said slowly and carefully. "The Americans are here to liberate us. The Germans are tired and hungry. My father says that if we can make the Germans think we're on their side, we can get out of this."

"I don't have time to wait for your father to work his magic with the Germans," she snapped. She turned and marched off into the snow, doing her best to put distance between herself and Antoine.

A howl rang out in the distant forest.

Juliette froze and felt thin fingers of ice stretching out along her veins. Where had it come from? She remembered the stories she'd heard as a child, about how wolves attacked people on the roads and hunted them down in packs.

She breathed hard out of her nose and stared straight ahead into the trees. She couldn't be scared now, especially in front of Antoine after she'd called him a coward. She would push forward. She had to be brave, for Papa and Mama. For Masha, and everyone else who was sick of being bullied and wanted their freedom back.

CHAPTER 13

They'd been running hard for a while when Boss heard the first gunshot and smelled the first whiff of carbine. She didn't stop but exchanged glances and barks with the rest of the pack, acknowledging they'd all noticed it.

The enemy.

They were close now.

Gregor began calling out to them in a softer voice, obviously trying to stay as quiet as possible. He had the dogs run for a while longer, but finally, after they crossed a wide, bright clearing and entered a new patch of thick woods, he pressed on the brake of his sled and called out to them, saying, "Whoa, whoa . . ."

Tank barked deep and loud, and they all came to a halt.

Boss's ears perked in excitement as Gregor walked down the line and untied them all, giving each one a Judy Junker's Tasty Treat as he went. They must have done a good job. But the fact that he was rewarding them for the first run meant that the second phase of their mission was at hand. And that was going to be tough.

Gregor went to the crates on the sled and began pulling out gray harnesses. They were similar to the ones the dogs wore now, only these were attached to packs full of supplies, tools, and anything else that might be needed to help the Allied troops. Boss and the pack had been trained in different smells. They'd learned which ones were friendly smells and which were enemy smells. The plan was to cross into enemy territory and bring these supplies to those with friendly smells. If they couldn't find any friendly soldiers, they had to look for normal humans from the area. Boss had smelled their food and fabrics, to identify them . . . but she couldn't be sure. They had to be careful around civilians. Humans were tricky that way.

It meant going alone, separated from Tank and the pack. Running through the woods, where anyone or anything could get at them. Only the best soldier dogs were chosen for this mission; Gregor needed the rest to help him mush the lightened sled.

"Boss," said Gregor. He came beside her, knelt, and helped her into a harness. She did her best to keep her tail still as he pulled it on; she wanted to look professional, even if she loved being chosen by Gregor.

The weight on Boss's shoulders felt good as Gregor secured her pack, but the dog's heart hurt. She knew this was the mission she was trained for, that it meant she was a good dog—but she also knew she might never see Gregor again. She'd never known a better human than him, one more like a dog in his soul.

Without thinking, she stepped forward and licked his cheek. Part of her was worried Gregor

would be upset, but instead he just smiled and petted her neck and said, "Good girl, Boss."

Gregor was finishing up Buzz's harness when the first voice hit Boss's ears. She gave a little *huruff*, and the other dogs in the pack all raised their heads and listened.

Humans, speaking the enemy language. Enemy shoe polish and tobacco smells.

They were near. She was sure of it.

Tank woofed softly at Gregor, and Gregor's head whipped around. All at once, Boss heard Gregor's heart begin to pound, and she smelled the first layer of fear sweat on his forehead.

The human's eyes ran over the dogs, and he nodded.

"Go," he said.

Boss wanted to give him one last nuzzle—but she didn't dare. That was for lazy dogs.

She turned to the woods and ran.

Snow billowed up around Boss as she leapt, and the forest gave way to a whole new array of sounds and smells—but this time, there was a new layer over it. For every cracking twig, there was distant gunfire and the crunch of enemy boots in the snow. For every whiff of pine and fleeing squirrel, there was an added hint of burning chemicals and sweating humans. It was war, all around them, and Boss knew that war meant she had to be on alert at all times. This was no hike with the pack—this was the mission, and it was do or die.

A gun fired. A yelp of pain rang through the air, followed by a bark of panic.

Boss stopped in a cloud of snow and turned to where the sound had come from.

She knew that voice.

She followed the panicked barking, picking up on smells along the way. There was fur, ration food, a backpack like hers . . . and blood, hot and fresh. She ran even faster, trying to ignore her fear as she picked up speed, and finally leapt over a rise to look down the other side.

Tank lay on his side in the snow, breathing fast, his leg wet with blood. Delta stood over him, whining with fear in her voice.

Boss rushed down the hill. She sniffed Tank's leg and got the basics—a cut, not very deep, definitely caused by a bullet. The enemy was nearby.

Far away but getting closer. Rifles.

Tank looked up at Boss, his face twisted in a whimper of pain and anger. He barked twice, sharply, telling both of them clear as day:

Go. Leave me.

Boss and Delta locked eyes. Neither of them could really believe it, but it was a direct order from their alpha: he wanted them to run while they had the chance.

The two dogs eyed one another, and without a single bark, Boss knew that she and Delta had the same thought:

Never.

They got on either side of Tank's harness, grabbed it with their jaws, and dragged him through the snow, Boss doing her best not to listen to Tank's whimpers of pain. Delta wanted to get him somewhere safe, like they'd learned to do with humans in training. Boss glanced around, looking for a big tree or even a cave—

Her nose picked up a sudden rush of smells—dirt, exposed roots, rotting leaves, mouse dens. A winning combination . . . if it wasn't too steep a drop.

They found the ditch a few feet away, and thankfully the slope was gentle, and they could manage. Carefully, Delta and Boss dragged Tank down the side and nestled him up against one of the dirt walls. He looked terrible, his leg still bloody, his breathing fast and shallow. Boss quickly licked his wound, hoping to clean it and let Tank know she was there for him. She shuddered at the sharp flavor of blood.

Boss turned to Delta. She still hated the other dog, but suddenly it didn't matter—it was as though their training instantly took over, guiding them through weeks and weeks of practice. Boss saw the same feeling grip Delta. They each had their job.

Delta was clever—she would cover the blood in case the enemy came by. Boss was fast—she would find help.

Boss ran out of the ditch and howled at the top of her lungs as she bounded off into the woods, hoping to draw the enemy to her and away from Tank.

She came over a hill and stopped dead in her tracks.

Two humans stood cold and surprised in the snow. They didn't smell like the enemy . . . but they were definitely afraid of her.

Boss crouched, ready for anything. Friend or foe—she'd find out.

CHAPTER 14

Juliette started with a cry and fell backward into the snow. The wolf loomed over her, its fur black and face white, its mouth open to reveal two jaws full of sharp teeth. It lowered its head and growled, sniffing the air around her. But it was those eyes, so blue they seemed to glow, like the eyes of a monster born from the snow, that made her gasp and shield her face.

She was so fascinated by the creature's eyes, she almost didn't notice the gray pack it wore strapped around its body. There was a row of three stars printed on its side.

Juliette barely had time to move. One moment, the wolf was walking over to her. The next, Antoine was running at the animal swinging a tree branch, yelling like a crazy person.

"Antoine, no!" she cried.

Once again, her speed saved them. Just as Antoine raised the branch overhead like a club, Juliette leapt between them and raised her arms, blocking the wolf from Antoine's blow. Antoine stopped short, nearly smacking her in the head with the branch.

"Get out of the way!" he cried, the wind taken out of his sails.

"It's not going to hurt us!" said Juliette with heavy breath. "It's an Allied wolf!"

Antoine stared at her like she had pigeons flying out of her ears. "It's a *what*?"

"Look," she said, and turned back to the wolf . . . or was it a dog? This close, Juliette could see that this animal was bigger and fluffier than any wolf she'd seen in books. Its bright eyes and triangular ears stood dramatically out of its white face. She'd seen dogs like these, in one of Mama's

movie magazines, posing with the actress Car-
ole Lombard. A *husky*, that was what they were
called.

When Juliette reached for the dog, it took a
tentative step back . . . then walked over to her.
Juliette was surprised that the dog wasn't scared—
after all, they could be Germans. She must be able
to tell the difference somehow.

Juliette pointed to the three stars on one side
of its harness, next to which was printed a single
word: *BOSS*.

"That star," she said. "It's a military symbol. I
think it means they're American."

"What's *Boss* mean?" said Antoine.

"I think it's her name," said Juliette.

"How do you know it's a she?" asked Antoine.

Juliette didn't think she could bring herself
to have that talk with Antoine right now, so she
turned her attention to the dog. She crouched
down and pet the dog's neck. "Boss?" she asked.
"Is that your name?"

In response, the dog whined and trotted away
from them. It turned back toward the woods, then
to them, then to the woods again.

Gunshots rang out in the distance. As they echoed through the forest, Boss woofed softly and trotted off between the trees. "Wait," said Juliette, climbing to her feet and running after the animal.

They crested the rise that Boss had stood on and looked down on a narrow ditch on the other side. A second husky, this one colored coppery red around the edges of its fur, danced around between the walls of exposed dirt, and a third lay at its feet, its one white leg stained with blood.

The children half walked, half slid down the rise and carefully inched their way into the ditch. Juliette knelt beside the injured husky, a big male with a backpack that said *TANK* on it. The poor dog's chest rose and fell quickly, and the blood on his leg stood out brightly against the snow and his white fur.

"He's been cut," said Juliette, feeling sick and scared, "or maybe shot. We have to stop the bleeding."

"How do we do that?" whispered Antoine, his eyes never leaving the dog's wound.

Juliette rolled her eyes, pulled off her scarf, and wrapped it around the dog's leg. The dog

whined and twitched as she pulled it tight around the wound, but he never snapped or barked at her. The other two dogs laid by and watched her attentively.

Another gunshot echoed throughout the woods, followed by voices yelling sharp orders in German. Juliette shared a glance with Antoine— the boy looked pale—and swallowed hard.

"What are we going to do?" she asked.

Antoine stared blankly ahead for a second . . . and then his eyes widened.

"I've got an idea," he said, and ran up out of the ditch. There was a loud crack, and Juliette was about to whisper at him to stop making so much noise, when Antoine returned with two long pine branches in his arms. He ran back down into the ditch and gently laid the pine branches over the dogs before pulling Juliette under a dark overhang of earth and crouching down in the shadows.

They stayed that way for an hour, the dogs quiet under the branches, Juliette and Antoine breathing down the necks of their coats to avoid creating steam with their breath. They listened as a squad of soldiers stomped through the trees above them, yelling at each other in German and occasionally firing off a gun. Juliette couldn't believe how quiet and subdued the dogs were. They had to be well-trained soldiers to be so silent.

Juliette wondered how many German soldiers had already reached Plainevaux. With this many in the woods, there was no question that they had finally started filtering into her hometown. Had her parents gotten out in time? She felt sick, thinking about how worried they must be, to go upstairs and find her gone. And what about everyone else in town? Was Alix all right? Were her family and friends being interrogated about a cabin in the woods where Jews were being hidden?

Finally, almost twenty minutes after they'd heard the last boots in the snow, Juliette and Antoine crept out from their hiding spot and uncovered the dogs. The two females, Boss and Delta—by her backpack—whined nervously and looked from the two of them to Tank and back again. Juliette felt her heart grow heavy in her chest as helplessness filled her. First Masha was gone, then the cabin was burned down, and now she couldn't help this beautiful wounded dog.

"I wish we could take him with us," she said, feeling a hot tear rush down her cheek. "If we leave him here, he's done for."

"It's . . . it's just as well," said Antoine. "These kinds of dogs are sled dogs. They need to pull heavy loads. With that injury, he might never pull a sled again."

"If only we had a way to carry him—hey!" cried Juliette. Boss had come up beside her and was nuzzling her hand and rubbing her harness roughly against Juliette's legs. She was about to shove her away when she felt a rough, bulging shape through the canvas of the backpack.

She realized what it was in an instant, and frantically began unbuttoning the flap on Boss's harness.

"What are you doing?" asked Antoine. "Careful, you don't know what's in there—"

"Rope!" cried Juliette, pulling a figure-eight bundle of rope out of the bag. She held it out to

Antoine triumphantly, the smile on her face so big it hurt her cheeks.

"Okay, you found rope," said Antoine, looking bewildered. "So what?"

"So," said Juliette, "I have a plan."

CHAPTER 15

"**M**ush!" said Antoine, lightly smacking Boss and Delta on the backside with a long branch.

"Cut that out," said Juliette. The exhaustion was finally getting to her, and she felt irritated at Antoine. "Why do you keep saying that?"

"I saw it in a newsreel with my father," said Antoine. "It's a sled dog term. They like it."

Juliette didn't think the dogs even noticed Antoine's weak whipping. The two female dogs seemed entirely focused on the job of dragging

Tank on the makeshift sled Juliette had pieced together from long strips of bark. She and Antoine had tied rope around the arm loops of Delta and Boss's harnesses so they could pull the sled. Tank looked better—his breathing had evened out, and his whining had stopped, but he still lay on his side with a hopeless look on his face. When they stopped to melt some snow and give the dogs the water from their cupped hands, Tank only lapped up a little before lowering his head.

Juliette understood how the wounded dog felt. She hugged her arms around her waist and tried to rub some warmth back into her body, but it was no easy task. The sun had set in the distance, and the temperature around them was dropping. She knew that soon it might even get down to negative degrees.

And they weren't even halfway to Lierneux yet.

"How much farther do you think it is?" she asked, trying not to let her teeth chatter. Knowing Antoine, he'd turn her exhaustion into an example of why girls were weaker than boys.

"A long way." Antoine sighed. "We're not even

at Chanxhe yet. We probably won't even make the river by midnight in this snow." He stopped, breathing heavily. "We might want to set up camp somewhere. It's getting late."

Juliette put her head down. "I'm not tired. We're going to keep moving forward until we get to Lierneux. That's where my parents wanted me to go."

Antoine sighed again but said nothing further. Juliette's spirits bucked up at his silence. He could sigh all he wanted; she was like Boss and Delta, brave and fearless, never giving up—

The sled dogs stopped in their tracks.

"Not you too," grumbled Juliette, turning and trudging back over to them. "What is it, dogs? We can't stop here, we have to keep moving."

Boss turned her snout up at the sky and sniffed. Then she looked down at Juliette with concerned eyes and whimpered.

Juliette was about to ask what was wrong when she felt a pinprick of cold against the back of her neck. She looked up to see fat flakes of snow drifting down all around them and thick gray clouds on the horizon.

"It's going to come down pretty hard soon," said Antoine.

"Then we have to gain ground while we can," said Juliette. "Come on."

She tried to get their party to move faster, but before they knew it, the snow flurries became a full-on storm. First, feathery flakes drifted slowly between the trees. Then they became swirling billows of white, and suddenly a diagonal pelting of wind-driven snow found its way into the neck of Juliette's jacket and so deep into her hair that she felt it on her scalp. When she looked down at herself, she saw that her coat and leggings were almost entirely white with the snow. Her fingers and feet were numb.

One of the dogs barked, bringing her back to the moment. Delta was tugging Boss off into the woods. Boss glanced at the kids and then began to follow Delta, dragging Tank with them.

"Wait!" cried Juliette, trudging back and trying to follow the dogs as best she could.

"Leave them!" cried Antoine, trying to shield his face from the blasting snow with his hand. "We've got to find shelter! We're going to freeze if we don't get inside soon."

Juliette couldn't argue with that. For a moment, she wondered if Antoine was right, if they should just leave the dogs and try to run in one direction as quickly as possible until they reached a town where they could beg someone for shelter. Then she heard both Boss and Delta barking steadily and loudly, and she realized the dogs knew something they didn't. Boss had shown her where her injured friend was *and* had shown her where the rope was in her pack—Juliette had a feeling she wasn't your typical sled dog.

Juliette followed the dogs, Antoine protesting but following behind her. Up ahead near a few thick pine trees, she saw one of the dogs prancing in the snow near a huge black opening beneath a heavy rock. The reddish husky, Delta, was gone, her rope leash discarded on the ground.

Boss barked and turned her head from Juliette to the cave and back again.

"You want us to go in there?" asked Juliette. "I don't know, girl, there might be a bear living in there—"

A *whuff* echoed out of the cave, and Delta trotted out, looking pleased with herself.

"Look at you, checking it out ahead of us!" Juliette laughed, feeling a little warmer than she had a moment ago. "Good girl! Come on, let's get inside."

CHAPTER 16

There it was again.

Boss lifted her head, twitched her ears, and listened. Definitely footfalls in the snow. She sniffed the air.

It was a deer. They were fine.

She lowered her head back to the floor and stared into the dying embers in the circle of stones. She was so tired, but she couldn't sleep. Every noise woke her, made her alert to the next fight she might run into, the next moment she might have to hide.

This mission was nothing like training.

In training, Boss had been one of the best. When Gregor had whistled, she had come, no matter how many mounds of snow or fallen trees had been in the way. When Gregor had taught her how to leap from the plane, she'd done so fearlessly, had landed perfectly, had immediately gotten into formation. When she'd been taken for a long hike and sent into the woods, she'd always found her way back. She was one of the best dogs in the pack, stationed right behind Tank in the line. A swing dog, one of the navigators. One of the smart ones.

But today, everything had gone wrong so quickly.

In her mind, she saw Tank the way she'd first seen him, over and over again: blood on his leg, his chest rising and falling fast, his eyes staring off in pain and helplessness. She'd never seen Tank that way before. Alphas should never look like that. She watched him now, asleep in one corner, his leg bandaged. He seemed peaceful—nothing like the Tank she'd seen earlier that day.

Boss huffed. They'd only been at war a few

hours, and already it was a fight to survive.

She heard a shifting beside her and saw eyes glitter in the darkness. Delta was awake, too; she'd probably heard the same deer. Boss had to admit, Delta had been a great help today. She wasn't always graceful, or powerful, and she was a long way behind Tank in the line. But she'd hidden Tank's blood from the enemy, and she had helped Boss pull Tank along without so much as a whimper. And she'd been good about helping the human pups, scouting out this hole in the ground before Boss even had a chance to sniff for big animals. There had been a bear with cubs in this cave—but they'd left seven or eight winters ago. The dogs could still smell them.

Delta had been good. For her place in line, she was a smart dog.

Boss narrowed her eyes. She had to stop thinking of the line. Tank was hurt, Delta was helpful, and Gregor was miles and miles away. They had been so worried about Tank that they'd entirely ignored their mission and were now probably way behind schedule. They had no line now, no mission, no pack.

The idea made her feel terribly lonely. No pack.

Or maybe not. She looked over to the two humans, sleeping nestled together like puppies trying to stay warm. They'd already been lucky enough to find pups—little humans who loved dogs and seemed to understand them better than most grown humans—but to have found such resourceful human pups, well, that was lucky. Not only were they friendly, they obviously wanted to get away from the enemy. And they'd helped Tank, even though they could've easily left him behind. Even though Gregor had taught them, his own dogs, to leave a wounded dog behind if they had to.

Boss liked them. The girl especially, with her round cheeks and big eyes. Juliette. Boss watched her now, shifting in her sleep, hugging her blanket tighter. Maybe she was a soldier after all—she was brave enough and knew the name of the base Gregor had taught them about. *Lierneux*. How could the human pup know, unless she'd been trained?

Maybe the line was gone. But Boss still had a pack.

✧ ✧ ✧

She awoke a few hours later, and carefully crept outside. She heard another crunch in the snow, beneath the whipping wind of the storm. She kept her ears alert. She might not sleep much tonight, but that was okay.

This sound was different. And the smell. The deer had moved on. This was the enemy.

Boss's ears perked. Her skin prickled, and the hair on the back of her neck went up.

A big group of enemy soldiers. Crunching through the snow, coming from the same direction as the human pups. Yelling to each other. Driving one of their big, smoky wagons across the countryside, filling the air with chemical smells and crashing noises.

Boss spun and ran back in the cave.

They needed to leave now.

CHAPTER 17

Juliette ran down the cobblestone streets, dribbling the ball with her feet as she went. The boys ran behind her, Antoine in the lead, all shouting and yelling that she wasn't allowed to do that, that girls weren't allowed to play soccer, but Juliette didn't care. She kept kicking the ball ahead, until the bakery was in sight, and she knew she was home free, that Papa and Mama would protect her from the mob of angry boys. But then the door opened, and instead of Papa, out stepped General Esser, his coat flapping around him like black wings and his eyes glowing red. He smiled and opened his mouth full of sharp teeth. As much as Juliette wanted to stop herself, she couldn't, she was still rushing toward him, even as he began—

Barking.

The noise yanked Juliette out of a deep, sound sleep. She lurched up to sit and gasped, trying to blink away her confusion as Antoine sat up behind her with a snort and mumbled, "What's . . . where . . . Papa?"

They lay in the cave they'd found last night, the fire long dead and the front entrance spilling white morning light in on them. Boss stood in front of her, anxiously but softly woofing, glancing between her and the entrance.

"What's got you so upset, girl?" mumbled Juliette, but even through the haze of sleep, she knew it didn't matter. Delta, the one with the reddish fur, was also standing and twitching nervously. Even Tank, who'd barely eaten the night before, was sitting halfway up and had his eyes wide open for the first time in a while.

"We have to go," said Juliette.

Antoine and Juliette quickly and quietly

dragged Tank out of the cave and got the dogs in their harnesses and rope leashes again. The fresh snow outside helped keep their movements quiet, but already Juliette could hear faint noises in the distance—voices, heavy footsteps, the rumble of a motor. They had no time to spare.

"Come on," said Antoine, pointing ahead. "The Ourthe River is maybe a mile or two in that direction. We can find a bridge across at some point—"

"It'll be frozen by now," said Juliette, bundling up in her coat and heading past him. "We can just walk across it."

"Rivers don't freeze all the way," snapped Antoine. "They're running water. Let me do the planning."

"Antoine, I don't have time for this," she said, feeling her anger at him give way to simple common sense. "If it were up to you, we'd be back in town getting questioned by the Germans. We'd have abandoned the dogs. My parents are in Lierneux, and the woods are full of Nazis, and this dog is hurt. So I'm going to Lierneux as fast as I can. If you feel like joining me, you're welcome to."

Juliette pushed onward, the dogs following behind her. She enjoyed Antoine's silence, but at the same time felt bad about how snippy she'd just been to him. It wasn't his fault that the Germans invaded. But nonetheless, she couldn't be bothered to waste time arguing with him about everything. She knew what she had to do.

She reached into her pocket and squeezed the wooden shape inside her cloth bundle. Her frustration melted away at the thought of Masha. What was she so upset about? She knew what she was running from, and she had somewhere to go. She had food and companionship (even if it was *Graubrot*, tinned fish, three dogs, and Antoine). But Masha was running with her family in a country where she was no longer welcome, where soldiers wanted to take her away for no other reason than her religion. She was probably out there now, walking through deeper snow than this, her big eyes filled with tears. Juliette should count her blessings.

She unwrapped the doll from its bundle and looked at its rough curves and half-carved face. She had a ways to go, but it wasn't that bad. It would be a nice present for Masha, a Hanukkah present.

Her mind flew back to Christmas, only a few days ago—cozy in their flat, wearing the new sweater Mama made her, Papa giving her a chocolate bar he'd been hiding away all day, listening to old Christmas records and singing along.

A smile crossed Juliette's face. The memories warmed her a little. She squeezed the doll tighter, and without thinking she began to hum beneath her breath.

"What are you singing?" asked Antoine.

A pang of rage struck Juliette, but she squeezed the doll a little tighter and thought of Masha. She had no right to be angry at Antoine for asking. "'The First Noel.' It's a Christmas carol."

"I know," mumbled Antoine.

Juliette went back to her humming. After a few minutes, she heard Antoine join in behind her. Something about it was nice; it made her feel a little less like she was a lost and lonely girl out in the woods. After the song was over, she switched to "Silent Night," and Antoine joined in on that one too. The dogs looked a little perplexed, and it made Juliette laugh.

The music made the time seem to go even faster, and before she knew it, Juliette could hear rushing water in the distance. She picked up the pace, and soon they were standing at the edge of the Ourthe River, with lines of snowy trees on either side of the rocky bank. The surface of the Ourthe was frozen over for the most part, but the ice looked thin and waxy, and big patches had melted away to reveal fast-running water.

Juliette imagined how cold that water was and shivered involuntarily. She wished there were a bridge they could use . . . but there was no time. They were still some thirty kilometers away from Lierneux, and Tank was looking worse.

"Well, it *is* frozen over," said Antoine, eyeing it. "But I'm not sure it'll hold. What do you think?"

Juliette stared at him, speechless. Had Antoine actually just asked for her opinion?

"I'm not sure," she said finally. "One of us can try, to see how thick it is."

Antoine nodded, and then something caught his eye, and a smile spread over his face. "Well,

I'll be," he said. "Look at that."

Delta stood at the edge of the river, testing the ice with her paw. Slowly but surely, she stepped out onto the frozen surface and stood there a moment . . . and it held! She trotted back over to Boss, and the two dogs each took a section of Tank's pine-bough sled in their teeth. They gently tugged it across the ice, and after only a few minutes and one slip by Delta, they were on the other side.

"Huh," said Antoine. "That's a good sign. I bet three dogs definitely weigh more than we do."

Juliette couldn't argue with him there. "Okay," she said, "but very carefully."

With small, sliding steps, Juliette edged out onto the surface of the river, Antoine following close behind. Juliette breathed slowly and steadily, trying to keep her fear at bay as every muscle in her body tensed. A third of the way across, they heard a deep, muffled cracking noise and stopped.

"Do you see any cracks?" asked Juliette.

"Not around me," said Antoine. "You?"

"No . . ."

Juliette took another step forward—and a

white line appeared in the ice next to her right foot.

"It's cracking," she said. She took a deep breath and blinked hard, trying to push back her fear. "On three, we're going to run, okay? We're going to just go for it."

"Wait," said Antoine in a shaky voice.

Juliette shook her head. No time to wait. "One," she said. "Two . . ."

On the other side of the river, the dogs began to growl.

Juliette looked up, startled. Boss and Delta crouched to protect Tank from a German soldier in a long black coat. His eyes were covered in goggles, his scarf was pulled up over his mouth and nose, and a rifle was strung across his back.

"Oh no," garbled Antoine. "What do we do?"

"I don't know," she said, feeling the silence of the woods around her, the terror of the standoff she now faced.

"We have to run," garbled Antoine. "We've got to—"

Juliette turned and watched as Antoine tried to retreat. She could almost see what was about to happen before it happened, like a fortune teller. She didn't know how she knew, she just knew.

Antoine's foot slipped and kicked out in front of him. For a moment, he was airborne—and then he crashed down onto the ice. There was a terrible splitting noise . . . then nothing.

Antoine laid perfectly still for a moment, then looked up at her and said, "I think we're okay."

"Whew," said Juliette, just before the ice beneath her gave way.

CHAPTER 18

Juliette never known cold quite like this.

The water bit her, wrapped tightly around her, stole every bit of feeling and warmth and breath in her body. She tensed and shook all over, shocked by the sudden drop in temperature.

She pumped her arms furiously, reached the surface—and her face collided with a solid sheet of ice. She slammed her fists against it, but it didn't budge.

No air. No heat. Trapped.

In her oxygen-deprived brain, one thought

remained: *It figures that Antoine slips and I'M the one who falls in.*

The current was powerful. The river rushed around her, soundless yet noisy, dragging her downstream. She felt dizzy, starved for air. Her vision grew dim, and she let herself be carried by the current. She hoped Antoine escaped the German. She hoped he saw Mama and Papa and the Kraismans again, and told Masha that Juliette had tried—

Something gripped the collar of her jacket and pulled.

Juliette croaked and gulped deeply as she emerged into the open air, which felt surprisingly warm compared to the freezing water. Boss and Delta pulled her from a hole in the surface, breathing hard as they dragged her backward onto the ice. The minute she was out of the water, both dogs began licking her face, their tongues blazing hot against her frozen skin.

"Are you hurt?" cried a voice in broken French. She turned to see the German trooper approaching her and pulling off his coat. A few feet away, the dogs spun and crouched, growling deep in their throats at him. The German froze and held out his coat at arm's length. Juliette edged away from him, not wanting to wear the long black coat that had become such a symbol of the Nazis . . . but she was freezing. Carefully, she rose, shuffled forward past the dogs, and let the soldier drape it around her. She had to admit, the big coat was warm, and helped cut her shivering and clicking teeth down immediately.

"Take this also," said the soldier in a familiar voice that made her shudder. "You'll freeze otherwise."

He unwound his scarf.

"I know you," she said.

It was Till, the soldier who'd helped burn down the cabin. The one who'd complained about the war. She gasped, wondering if he was out here with his troop, and if Gerhardt or General Esser would find them and recognize her.

Till wrapped his scarf over her head, then held her out at arm's length and smiled.

"Let's get you in front of a fire," he said. "Come on."

Juliette tried to walk, but she couldn't move

her legs. Her muscles ached from the cold, and her limbs were still numb. She made a whimpering noise, and Till seemed to understand. He put one arm around her shoulders, swept his other under her knees, and carried her toward Antoine and the dogs.

"Is she dead?" cried Antoine. "Is she hurt?"

"To my fire, quickly," said Till. "Bring your dogs if you must." And then he set out into the woods, with Antoine and the dogs following close behind.

CHAPTER 19

Boss kept her head low and her ears up as she pulled Tank after the human pups. She side-eyed Delta and knew instantly that her packmate had the same idea. The minute the enemy tried to pull anything, they'd be ready. If he even looked at the pups wrong, Boss would attack.

She snorted. In the air, she could smell smoke and wood, old rations and enemy boot polish.

Going to the enemy's camp. What was *wrong* with these human pups?

If only they could smell the danger in the

enemy that Boss and her pack had been taught to recognize. If only they could feel how sick the enemy's stench made them, how every inhale of the enemy was a slap to the muzzle. It wasn't their fault; dogs knew that human noses and ears were terribly inadequate. But they also hadn't received the training that Boss and Delta had. That was why they'd been able to save Juliette from the water. Boss and Delta were good dogs, meant to be soldiers.

Then again . . . the enemy had helped. He had saved the female, Juliette. Maybe that counted for something.

They reached the camp, a shoddy setup around a smoldering fire. The smells of the place overwhelmed Boss—everything stunk of the enemy, from the clothing to the metal on the kettle hanging over the fire. The raw scent of forbidden goods made her choke slightly, and she and Delta stopped before reaching the edge of the fire. Boss could feel the heat and knew that it would feel nice to lie next to the flames . . . but she hadn't been trained as a soldier only to give in to the enemy the moment he offered them a treat.

The enemy soldier handed Juliette clothes and pointed toward his tent. As she headed over, he gestured to the dogs and spoke to Antoine, the boy pup. He answered back, and Boss caught a few words. Mainly *Tank*.

The enemy soldier went over to a bag by the fire and brought out a small green box. Even before he reached them, Boss could smell what was inside: chemicals, bandages, metal tools. A box like the one Gregor had used on Boss when she'd scraped her leg on a nail and needed stitches.

The enemy soldier walked quickly toward them.

Without thinking, Boss and Delta were on their feet, growling. The soldier stopped dead, raising one hand. The fur on Boss's neck prickled. What was this human thinking, walking at them so fast? Did he think they wouldn't attack him? The nerve!

Antoine darted out in front of the enemy soldier and said some human words. Boss and Delta picked some of them—*Tank. Injured. Help.* Antoine pointed to the box, then to Tank.

Boss woofed nervously. She understood, she

just hated the thought of the enemy laying hands on Tank. She glanced at Delta, though, and saw that her packmate had different ideas. Her eyebrows and back fur told Boss that Delta was more afraid of Tank staying hurt than she was of the enemy.

Delta had been helpful so far. She may be clumsy, but she was dedicated to the pack.

Boss moved aside and let the enemy soldier through.

Tank growled low and whined as the enemy soldier rubbed chemicals on his wound and stitched it up, but he was in no position to attack. And anyway, Boss and Delta stood on either side of the enemy, ready to strike at any moment.

Eventually, the enemy soldier stood and backed away, and Boss and Delta gave Tank's wound a sniff. It did smell cleaner than it had before and looked less ugly and worrisome now that it was stitched up. Tank even sat up and gave it a light lick before laying back down. At least in this situation, thought Boss, he would be saved the humiliation of wearing a cone around his neck to keep him from licking the wound or biting at his stitches.

She and Delta laid down next to Tank and shared a look. Perhaps this enemy soldier wasn't so bad after all. She'd let him off the leash for now.

Boss huffed a breath. Delta returned it. They both understood.

If he made one wrong move, he was dog food.

CHAPTER 20

Juliette pulled the blankets close in around herself and hunched against the itchy material of the long underwear she now wore. The fire felt good on her face, and the tin mug warmed her hands. She sipped the weak tea inside, wincing at the flavor—terrible, like it had gone bad!—but savoring its heat. She passed the cup to Antoine, who silently took it and sipped without ever taking his eyes off of the figure across from them.

On the other side of the campfire sat Till. Between Juliette's clothes on the big sticks planted in the ground where they hung drying, the Nazi silently watched them as he poured himself a cup of tea from his camping kettle. He eyed the children warily; Juliette thought he looked as scared of them as she felt of him. Behind him sat the green triangle of his tent. Boss and Delta laid farther off, snuggling up against Tank to warm him. They'd refused to enter the Nazi's campsite, even after he'd stitched up Tank's wound. Juliette couldn't help but wonder if they'd had the right idea.

But Till didn't seem cruel, Juliette thought. He'd saved her life and given her dry clothes. He'd helped Tank. How could a man so in league with an evil cause have any good inside him?

"Where are you two heading?" asked the soldier in heavily accented French.

"Say nothing," whispered Antoine.

Till's face looked hurt for a moment, but then he stretched his lips tight and nodded. "Smart boy. That's wise." He stared into his cup and sighed. "You are afraid of me, aren't you?"

"Yes," said Juliette.

Till nodded. He reached into his pocket and

held a scrap of red fabric out to Juliette—a Nazi armband, obviously removed from his coat. He smoothed out the fabric so she could see the jagged black swastika in the white circle.

"Because of this?" he asked.

"Yes," said Juliette.

"Because of what you've done," said Antoine. "Because of what *all* Nazis have done to our country and to our friends."

Till looked at Antoine, then down at the armband. "To the *world*," he said softly. A fat tear rolled down his cheek and plopped onto the toe of his hunting boot.

The hunting boot jarred Juliette's mind awake. It was brown leather and fur-lined, nothing like the pitch-black combat boots worn by Nazi soldiers. Bit by bit, she put little clues together. The armband in the pocket, not on the coat. The itchy long underwear he had given her, obviously made by a mother. The tent, a simple canvas model—one bought at a store before a big hike, not a single swastika on it. The far side of the Ourthe, away from the German front as it made its way south through Plainevaux. His complaints earlier in the cabin, about missing his free will, about not knowing who he was fighting for.

"You're a deserter," said Juliette.

Till looked her in the eye and nodded. "This morning," he said softly, "I . . . I burned down somebody's home."

Juliette wanted to blurt out, *We know*, but managed to keep her mouth shut.

"And for some reason, that act made me think about everything I've done," said Till, staring into the flames. "All of the people I've hurt, the lives I've destroyed. All for my country. And that's only me—not to mention what I've heard is going on outside of Belgium.

"And I . . . couldn't take it anymore," he said, his voice cracking. "I ransacked a supply shed, paid a family in town for clothes and camping gear . . . and left. Whatever happens now, it happens because of me. Not because of Germany, or Hitler, but because I want it to."

"And what if you get caught?" asked Antoine. "What if you're asked to pay for your crimes?"

"Then it will be deserved," said Till. He looked up to the overcast sky and sighed. "Something tells me I will have to answer for them eventually. But maybe not here."

They sat for a moment longer, the only sound the crackling of the fire. Eventually, Till took off one of his gloves, sat forward, and squeezed Juliette's clothes where they dangled.

"They're dry," he said. "You should get going."

Juliette gathered her clothes, went into the tent, and changed back into her dress and leggings. She reached into the pocket of her jacket and exhaled with relief as she felt the cloth-wrapped bundle of the doll inside of it. When she came out of the tent, Antoine was wrapping Tank in one of Till's blankets. Boss and Delta never took their eyes off Till, and the hair on their backs never lowered.

"Goodbye," said Juliette softly.

"Bun anay," said Till.

"What?" asked Juliette.

The soldier cleared his throat, and said in slow, careful French, *"Bonne année.* Happy New Year."

Juliette nodded and headed off into the woods with Antoine and the dogs. She looked back once more, just in time to see Till throw his armband in the fire.

CHAPTER 21

Boss trotted up to the head of the party, Delta flanking her perfectly. They didn't even need to exchange a glance to let the other know what they were thinking. They were both so confused by the human's actions that it was painted all over their muzzles.

Maybe the same foolishness that had let Juliette and Antoine get won over by the enemy soldier was the same thing that had made the soldier help them. The sense of kinship. The feeling that they were all one pack.

Then again, he'd helped Tank. She looked back at her alpha and saw his eyes wide open and his breathing steady, even if he wasn't moving much. It was undeniable—the enemy's stitches made him feel better. He'd even given Tank a blanket, something enemy troops weren't in the habit of doing.

Boss huffed. It was still nonsense. It would get them in trouble if they didn't watch their backs. But it had helped them this time.

They broke through the tree line and into a clearing in the woods, where the forest hills sloped down into a valley before rising up into another hill, and more thick forest. A road ran along the bottom of the valley, winding around the hills until it went out of sight. At least this clearing, thought Boss, was exposed to the sun and would be a little less snowy than the forests they'd been trudging through. Boss loved snow and felt alive in it, but for human pups, it was slow going. She missed Gregor and the rest of the pack. She hoped they were safe somewhere, away from the enemy, warming themselves by the fire.

For the first time since she'd left the pack,

Boss wondered if she'd ever return. Maybe not. Maybe that was okay—that the pack got to safety, even if she didn't. Her job was to help humans who needed her, and she was doing that. If she never saw the pack again, well . . . it would hurt. But she had done her job. That's what good dogs did.

She put her nose down and began searching for new smells. Not the pack, but smells that would help them—friendly gunpowder, friendly clothing. A town, a base, anywhere they could go. This was her job now, getting them somewhere safe.

Delta whined, and Boss noticed her sniffing the air. She raised her muzzle, took in a deep breath.

Enemy clothing and bullets, definitely. There was a noise, too, a thin slicing sound that she had heard around the camp before, but which she'd never quite locked down to a specific source . . .

A new smell filled Boss's nostrils. A familiar smell.

Wait . . . could it be?

From around one hill, a black-and-white

smudge darted along the road and ran as fast as it could. Even this far off, Boss recognized the lolling tongue and graceful gait of her packmate and line neighbor, Buzz.

Racing after Buzz were two enemy soldiers in thick black-and-white uniforms. They glided over the snow on thin pieces of wood that were strapped to their feet, pushing themselves along with spiked poles they dug into the ground. Boss remembered seeing these long snow gliders stacked up in the front room of their pen back at the base. Gregor never wore them, but some of the other soldiers took them when they went out on missions. So *that* was what they were for . . .

Though Buzz was fast, the enemy were gaining thanks to their snow gliders. Boss loved Buzz, but she was built more for endurance than speed. And though she was keeping a steady pace, the enemy was gaining on her.

Boss looked at Delta. Delta growled and nodded.

So much for camouflage.

The two dogs lowered their heads and scratched

at the ropes around their necks until they slid over their heads. Boss barely heard Juliette's protest as she and Delta bounded down the hill, running full speed toward the enemy soldiers.

Boss was faster than Delta and reached the closest soldier just as he drew his rifle from his back and pointed it at Buzz. The man looked up from his aim only a split second before Boss launched herself from the ground.

BAM! Boss slammed into the enemy soldier's side and knocked him to the snow. The minute he fell, she stood up over him and revealed her teeth to his face in a show of dominance. She growled and raised her back hair to let him know she was serious. Behind her, Delta had bitten onto the other soldier's arm and dragged him to the ground with a cry.

The enemy soldiers both held up their hands . . . but their eyes weren't focused on the dogs' teeth. They went elsewhere, farther down the road . . .

Boss heard the thin slicing sound again.

More snow gliders!

Boss felt the cold creep beneath her coat and into her skin. She was outnumbered.

The third enemy soldier slid to a halt a few feet away from them.

He eyed the dogs for a moment, and then drew his rifle and aimed it at Boss.

CHAPTER 22

Juliette and Antoine saw the third soldier winding down the road before the dogs did. Once again, Juliette's quick mind put together what was about to happen. But this time, for once, Antoine didn't need her to say it out loud. It was like how the dogs seemed to know what the other was thinking—suddenly they were both on the same page.

"Let's go," said Antoine.

They bolted down the hill, Juliette loving how well they could run now that there was less snow.

The growling of the dogs and the sound of the soldier's skis drowned out their footsteps, until they crouched behind a tree near the Nazi ski trooper just as he stopped and drew his gun.

Antoine was quick—he gathered up a handful of snow and packed it tightly.

"HEY!" he shouted.

The soldier froze and looked up at them.

Antoine pitched the snowball right into the soldier's face. The ski trooper reeled, windmilling his arms, and finally flopped hard onto his back. His head bounced against the ground with a *THUD* that made Juliette wince, and then the Nazi lay back and gave a dazed moan.

In an instant, Juliette crouched on top of the soldier. Energy and anger raced through her. She snatched the whittling knife from her bundle, brought it out, and pointed it at the Nazi's face. The first thing the soldier saw when he wiped his goggles clean was her blade inches from his face.

"Little girl," he said in clipped French, "put that knife away—"

"Why, so you can shoot me?" she shouted. "So you can kill me, like you planned to kill this poor dog? Or so you can take me away like you took my friends and neighbors?"

The ski trooper scowled. "This is war," he said.

"You're right," she said, jabbing the knife forward. "Maybe I should just—"

"No!" cried the ski trooper, putting up his hand.

"No," she said finally. "I'm not like you. I won't take your life." A smile sprouted on her face. "But we will take your skis. Antoine, go get the rope."

Slowly but steadily, they tied the Nazis' hands behind their backs and their legs together using lengths of the rope Juliette cut off with her whittling knife. They weren't perfect bonds—the soldiers would probably wriggle out of them in an hour or two. But they'd hold long enough for her and Antoine to get away. The dogs stood by the troopers, growling into the soldiers' frightened faces as Antoine and Juliette tied them up. Juliette wondered if the huskies looked like wolves to the soldiers, and Antoine and she appeared to be feral children living out in the wild.

They gathered the ski equipment and split it up between them—a pair for Juliette, a pair for

Antoine, and a pair for Tank to slide on. Juliette's were huge and unwieldy, and the foot straps fit loosely, but she managed to get them tied securely enough. She'd never skied before, and fell twice, but Antoine lifted her up both times. Eventually she got the hang of the poles. Both she and Antoine tied one of their poles to Tank's new sled and pulled him along as they slid their way across the countryside, Boss, Delta, and the new dog, Buzz, bringing up the rear and occasionally giving Tank a nudge with their heads.

As the wind whistled past her ears, Juliette looked out at the snowy countryside rushing past her and wondered how she'd gotten this far in so short a time. One moment, she was stealing bread from her own family and worrying that the Kraismans would get caught by the Nazis; the next, she was ambushing German soldiers and racing across Belgium on a cross-country ski trip.

She also noticed something had changed in Antoine. He no longer mocked her or got snippy with her. When she had trouble with her skis, he was patient. And when he had trouble with his skis, he asked for help. She could see that he was

still having a hard time not criticizing her at every turn—there were several moments where his face would scrunch up, but he always stayed quiet. Maybe nearly dying on the ice had changed his mind about what was important.

She stopped herself. Those were worries for when they were safe. And besides, the events of the last two days were clouding her mind. Of course Antoine seemed nice while they were trapped in the forest together, because he wasn't one of the many people actively trying to kill her. But he was the same boy who'd talked about her as though she were an insect two days before, and whose father made merry with the Nazi officers she'd seen around town. This was war, not real life. She shouldn't get the two mixed up.

"I recognize that farmhouse," said Antoine, pointing into the distance.

"Good," she said, still unable to shake the worry that she was only seeing the Antoine he wanted her to see out in the woods.

The forest soon grew thicker, and the paths between the trees got narrower. Juliette and Antoine abandoned the skis, kicking snow over them and their poles so the Nazis wouldn't find them. They decided to keep Tank on his skis because it was easier to move him around, and Juliette and Antoine pulled him with two remaining ski poles.

They had been walking for an hour, and Juliette was beginning to sweat with the effort of pulling the prone dog around trees and roots, when they all heard the bark.

Juliette and Antoine imitated Boss, Buzz, and Delta, raising their heads up and listening to the stillness around them. Had they imagined it? Boss barked . . . and another bark answered her.

From out in the woods came a howl. The huskies tilted their heads back and answered it, and soon even Tank was howling from his spot on his sled. Watching the majestic dogs, so much like wolves, howling into the forest, was both exciting and a little spooky.

All at once, Boss, Buzz, and Delta bolted into the forest, disappearing in a flash.

"Wait!" cried Juliette, reaching out as though she could grab the dogs and stop them. She tried to run after them, but between the snow and cold, her typical speed and nimbleness just wasn't there. A few yards out, she felt Antoine's arm wrap around her waist and stop her.

"We need to go after them," she cried, struggling against his grip. "They might get lost."

"They know what they're doing," said Antoine. "Those other dogs might be dangerous. They could be enemy hounds. Besides, we can't leave Tank alone out here."

Juliette wrenched free of his grip and turned to Antoine. She felt sad at how quickly Boss and Delta had disappeared. All of her feelings surged up to the surface as she looked at Antoine's arrogant face.

"Don't tell me what to do," she said.

"Tank could die if we leave him out here alone!" said Antoine.

"Then *you* stay with him, and I'll go after them," she said.

"What if you get lost out there? Or run into enemy hunting dogs?" he said. "You could get hurt, and then it'd just be me trying to pull Tank on my own!"

"Oh, shut up," she snapped. "You think you're

always right, but you're just a bully whose father buddies up to the Nazis while the rest of us try to survive!"

She felt bad the minute she said it. She could see on Antoine's face how the comment had stung him—a wince of pain shot across it, and his eyes glistened with tears. For once, it wasn't his fault either—she'd just worked herself into a bad mood thinking about the war and the Antoine she used to know. The fiery anger that had just filled her suddenly washed away and was replaced by regret and disappointment with herself.

"Fine," he said, turning back toward the way they came. "Go chasing after the dogs. I'm going to stay with Tank and see if I can pull him with only one ski pole."

He stormed off toward where they'd left Tank. Juliette felt torn in two—did she chase the dogs and leave Antoine, or help him look after Tank while Boss and Delta ran off to who knows where?

"*Mon dieu.*" She sighed and stomped off after Antoine. "Antoine, wait, I'm sorry I—"

She rounded a tree and froze.

Antoine stood still a few yards from Tank's sled. Next to the sled crouched a man in a white uniform and goggles. When he saw Juliette, he rose slowly to his feet. She could see the gun clasped in his one hand.

After all their effort, they'd been caught.

CHAPTER 23

Boss, Delta, and Buzz ran through the woods, trying to catch the thin wisps of scent out in the snowy forest.

It had to be around there somewhere. Boss's nose didn't just make things up, it was trained by the army. She raised her head again and barked, and another bark answered them.

There, closer, off between those two trees.

The three dogs leapt through the snow, following the echoing noise. Boss's lungs burned, and she breathed heavily and loudly as she pushed herself farther and farther through the forest.

Almost . . . there . . .

They burst into a clearing . . . and there it was! The sled! The other six dogs! The line! The pack!

For a moment, all of the dogs lost their training and joyously collided with each other. Boss, Delta, Buzz, and their other packmates all leapt in the air and barked excitedly, not caring who heard them.

The supplies! The sled! Gregor's mission was still incomplete, but now Boss, Delta, and Buzz were back and ready to help. There was still time, still hope! It wasn't all human pups and enemy soldiers; now, Gregor could—

Boss stopped mid-leap and whined. Gregor. Where was Gregor? Had he made it to Lierneux?

The rest of the pack whined back and looked around. They didn't know. He'd been here recently. He'd only just left. And now—

A cry rang out in the forest. Thin, high-pitched. Young.

Boss and Delta's eyes locked. The human pups.

How could they have gotten so distracted?

The two of them rushed back into the snow, barreling between the trees, hoping to reach the pups before their new hope was totally lost.

CHAPTER 24

Juliette thought her heart must be pounding loud enough for the strange man to hear. She felt as though this moment, with the three of them standing silently in the snow, lasted for minutes, hours, days. Blood rushed in her ears as she wondered whether the soldier would take them away . . . or just shoot them where they stood.

There was a rush of wind at their sides as Boss and Delta leapt back through the trees. The two dogs barked as they rushed at the strange new figure.

The figure raised his hand—and the dogs stopped and sat attentively.

Juliette's eyes bulged. What was going *on* here?

The new figure laughed from underneath the scarf that covered his mouth. He crouched and opened his arms, and Boss and Delta ran into them, licking him all over his face and nuzzling his neck. He laughed even louder, and softly said their names, "Boss, Delta!"

"What's going on?" whispered Juliette from the corner of her mouth.

"Look," said Antoine. He pointed to the soldier's arm, and Juliette saw the same three stars symbol printed there as was stamped on the dogs' harnesses. An American soldier, then—one of the Allies now entering the Ardennes. "I . . . think he's their owner."

The soldier stepped forward and removed his scarf, revealing a beard flecked white with frost and a big, warm smile. He excitedly asked them something . . .

In English.

"Do you speak any English?" asked Antoine.

"No," admitted Juliette. "Just French, some

Flemish, and some German."

"Excuse me, sir," asked Antoine politely in French, "do you speak French?"

"Yes," said the man with a smile. "A little. My mother is was in a Canada, and there is a lot of French in Canada. You have my dogs known! And friend Tank is to hurt but is found you with!"

"Oof," mumbled Antoine, "that's some bad French."

"Yes," said Juliette. "You are Boss and Delta's person, right? You brought them here."

"I did!" said the American. He extended a hand, and Juliette and Antoine each warily shook it. "Gregor Thomas. I to be the . . . how do you say *musher* in French?"

"I think I understand," said Juliette. "You have a sled, yes?"

"Yes," he said, "only there's been a problem. Well, come and see . . ."

Gregor led them through the forest and to a small clearing where Gregor's sled, which looked like someone had stopped midway through building a model of a shoe, sat in the snow, piled high with crates. Six huskies were tied to the front, who excitedly barked at Boss and Delta as they trotted over. When Antoine and Juliette dragged Tank over, the dogs all got excited, and actually pulled the sled forward a few feet to sniff around him. He must be their leader, thought Juliette, or something like it.

Gregor pointed to the one runner on the sled. It was cracked in the center, an accident he related to a huge rock jutting out of the snow a few feet away.

"I must make supplies to American soldiers," he said. "They stand hurt in Lierneux."

Juliette's heart leapt. "We're going to Lierneux!" she said. "What can we do to help?"

"Well, my sled made to well must be," said Gregor.

"What about the skis?" said Antoine, pointing to the sled they'd constructed for Tank. "Could we tie them on and use them as a makeshift runner?"

Gregor's smile shot up again, and he cackled and slapped Antoine on the arm. "Very smart, boy son! Very smart! Here we to go!"

Juliette and Antoine helped tie the skis to the

runner of the sled so they sat beneath the crack. The sled was a little lopsided as a result, but they gave it a practice push and it seemed movable. As they worked, Juliette and Antoine used a mix of French, German, and hand motions to explain to Gregor what they'd been through the past couple of days. The American soldier seemed amazed that two children could escape a burning cabin and rob Nazi troops of their skis.

They helped Gregor load Tank into the cargo basket of the sled and tie Boss and Delta at the front of the line. Gregor examined Tank's wound and nodded approvingly at the stitches. Apparently, thought Juliette, Till had known what he was doing. Then they all stood on the foot boards in a line, with Juliette pressed up against the handle, Antoine behind her, and Gregor reaching over them.

The American whistled and yelled something in English . . . and they were off!

CHAPTER 25

Boss felt the weight of the entire pack on her harness. She felt the snow billowing up in her face, whipping past her without a hint of another dog's scent in her nostrils. She saw the entire landscape laid out in front of her, the path between the trees coming to her as if by instinct. She'd always thought taking the front of the line would be terrifying, but now she was taking to it easily.

Her heart swelled with pride. She couldn't believe it. She was lead dog.

At her side, Delta powered forward as well,

doing her part to steer and haul the new weight. Boss thought about how only a day ago, she would have been disgusted to have been stationed next to Delta, just a team dog who was too clumsy to pull the sled. How things had changed. Though she missed having Buzz at her side—Buzz was in the back next to Dash, who was too concerned about Tank to lead—Boss was proud to run alongside Delta.

She forced herself to stop thinking and focus on the task at hand. She had her pack back, she had Gregor and the human pups in tow . . . but they weren't safe. Not yet. All around her, Boss could hear and smell the enemy. Their guns popped, their soldiers screamed and shouted, their heavy machines rolled across snow in an endless crunch. She caught whiffs and sounds that were promising too—friendly soldiers, friendly machines—but they were still in enemy territory. One wrong move, and Boss could lead the whole pack right into an enemy base.

Delta barked encouragement to her. Boss nodded and hunkered down, using every muscle in her body as hard as she could. She barked to the rest of the pack and heard them bark back at her.

They had miles to go. But they would get to Lierneux. They would complete the mission.

Or die trying.

CHAPTER 26

Juliette squinted and laughed as the cold wind blew in her face. Skiing had been one thing, but this, riding along with dogs pulling them, was unbelievable. It was as though they were flying over the ground as they zipped through the countryside—until a bump or hill would fling the sled into the air for a moment and make Juliette feel as though her stomach were rising up into her throat.

She reached into her pocket and squeezed the doll tightly in her hand, hoping to pull some bravery from it. They were almost there. The

Germans were still all around them . . . but this was at least faster than walking.

Behind her, Antoine was completely silent, and she could feel by the stiffness of his arms gripping the handle and his heartbeat through her back that he was scared to death. But Gregor didn't seem in the least bit worried about their speed, and simply laughed and occasionally called out to the dogs.

"How far out are we?" called Juliette to Antoine. Antoine said nothing. "Antoine? How far—"

"Leave me alone," Antoine said sullenly. Juliette lowered her head and felt a pang of shame come over her. He obviously hadn't forgotten the things she'd said to him earlier.

After an hour or so, they left a patch of woods, and Lierneux came into view in the distance, a smattering of farmhouses and spired municipal buildings sprawled out black and gray along the white snow-covered hills.

"Look!" cried Juliette. "There it is! Lierneux!"

Smoke drifted lazily from its chimneys, mixing with the overcast sky, and yet to Juliette, the sight of the little burg was more beautiful than anything she'd ever seen. Even this far out, Juliette could hear noises in the distance—engines and motors, the honking of a horn. She hoped that those were Allied vehicles, that the city wasn't teeming with Germans, and that Mama and Papa had made it there alive.

As they reached the edge of town, Gregor called out to the dogs and instructed Juliette to press down on the brake pedal at her feet. The dogs slowed to a halt just outside of a tall, pointed church on a corner. No sooner had they gotten off the sled than a huge green transport truck roared out from behind the church and pulled up right in front of the sled, causing the dogs to bark and jump in agitation.

A soldier in green leapt out of the transport, and Juliette's heart thudded in her chest . . . until the soldier spoke English, and she saw the letters *US* on the chest of his uniform. Mama and Papa had been right—Lierneux was safe.

Gregor laughed, walked over, and spoke to him in English. He gestured to Antoine and Juliette and mentioned their names a few times.

The American nodded and yelled something at the transport. More soldiers piled out and began taking the crates from Gregor's sled and tossing them into the back of their truck. Meanwhile, the American soldier waved the kids toward the church, and in broken French said, "I am believe you are to be the expected."

"Oof, I guess they don't teach French in America," mumbled Antoine.

Juliette's heart was aching to see her family and friends—but she couldn't just leave her traveling companions. She walked one by one to the dogs and put her arms around their necks, burying her face in each of their fur. She got to Boss last and squeezed the big husky so tight that the dog gave out a little grumble.

"Goodbye, my friends," said Juliette, tears pricking her eyes. "Thank you for everything. I'll see you soon."

Inside the church, pews had been cleared away and stacked against the walls to make room for cots. All around stood dozens and dozens of people, many of whom Juliette recognized from Plainevaux. From across the room, Luca Diget waved awkwardly at her.

Juliette spun, looking around the room. Had they made it? Were they here? Did they—"

"Juliette!"

Mama's voice.

Juliette turned in time to see Mama and Papa running toward her. Before she even knew what was happening, tears sprang up in Juliette's eyes, and she sprinted across the room and slammed into their arms so hard she made the wind fly out of Papa. She wept, finally, pouring out all the fear and cold and madness of the past few days.

"Never run off like that again," cried her mother through sobs.

"I'm sorry," gushed Juliette. "I came here as fast as I could. I was worried you'd come looking for me." She pulled back and looked into their faces. Even Papa's cheeks glistened with tears. "What happened? Is everyone okay?"

"People in town saw smoke rising from the forest and knew something was wrong," said Mama. "Mr. Marzen came and helped us get safe passage to Lierneux, and then sent out a search party to find you—"

"Antoine's father?" asked Juliette. "But . . . I thought he was friends with the Nazis."

Papa looked puzzled. "Not at all. He only pretends so he can know what they're planning and find who in their ranks wants to desert. Antoine's mother and father have saved us more times than I can remember. They're out there now, helping the Americans stage their next attack."

Juliette looked back across the room. Antoine sat on a cot, his head hung down, looking very alone in the world. Part of her thought she should go over and say sorry when a little form ran across the room and leapt into Antoine's arms. The sight of her made Juliette's breath catch, and she sprinted over to greet them.

"Masha?" she asked.

The little girl looked up from hugging Antoine and gave Juliette a big smile full of baby teeth. "Juliette!" Masha cried as she hugged her. Juliette squeezed the little girl as hard as she could. Masha pulled back and stared at Juliette with bright, excited eyes.

"Everyone is talking about you," she said. "They said you and Antoine escaped a burning building and took out a whole squadron of Germans on skis! One of the soldiers is saying that if you hadn't helped fix that man's sled, there'd be no food left here for us. You're heroes!"

"I don't know about that," said Juliette with a laugh. "But we did get to run with some beautiful dogs. Do you want to come meet them?"

Masha gasped and nodded. Juliette forced herself to turn to Antoine, smile, and say, "Do you want to come with us?" The boy looked surprised, but then nodded and rose. The three of them ran off together.

CHAPTER 27

That night, the Americans set up a long communal table in one part of the church, and they all ate dinner there together, both the refugees from Plainevaux and the American soldiers helping them. It wasn't a fancy meal—just onion soup, with bread and cheese—but they were all grateful to eat it and smiled warmly at each other as they passed down plates. Mama and Papa sat on Juliette's left, while Masha and her family sat on her right.

Antoine's mother and father showed up

midway through the meal—they'd been helping get the last of the people harboring Jews out of Plainevaux before the Nazis began interrogating any of them—and had a tearful reunion with their son. Both Mr. and Mrs. Marzen had smudges of dirt on their hands and faces, and said they'd had to hide out in their root cellar while the Germans tore their house apart.

"The town is entirely overrun with Nazis," said Mrs. Marzen as she sat down at the table. "But they're hungry, and scared. The rumor is that they got too confident early on in the battle, and now they're without supplies."

"Will we ever be able to go back?" asked Mama.

"If we had to guess, within the month," said Mr. Marzen putting his arm around his son. "But let's not worry about that now. What matters is, we're alive and together."

Everyone sat and listened as Antoine recounted their story yet again, and Juliette couldn't help but admire Antoine's wording, even if it was a little embellished.

"The soldier's not on the ground for a moment

when Juliette's on his chest with a knife in his face," said Antoine. "She looks down at him, and she says, *Merry Christmas, I'd like my country back.*"

The mention of Christmas sent sparks in Juliette's mind. She reached into her coat pocket and brought out the doll she'd carved for Masha.

"Here," she said, pressing it into the little girl's hands. "I made this for you. I know it's not very good, but . . ."

Masha gasped and clutched the doll to her chest. "I love it!" she cried. "It's so beautiful. No one's ever made me anything like . . . I didn't . . ."

Masha leaned in and hugged Juliette again. Juliette held her tightly, and she felt the little girl begin to shake in her arms. After a few moments, Juliette realized she was crying, and saying "thank you" over and over. Juliette's own eyes stung, and suddenly hot tears ran down her cheeks as she held Masha tighter and rocked back and forth with her.

She didn't know why she started singing—she thought it was to comfort Masha, but she knew it was more than that. She felt full of it, full of warmth and comfort and most of all hope. If she could get Masha her doll, then there was hope yet—for Belgium, for Europe, for the whole world. Without thinking, "Silent Night" came from her lips. At first, everyone around her went quiet and stared at her, one or two of the adults mumbling that Christmas was over. Juliette got ahold of herself and stopped only for Antoine to join in across the table on "Sleep in heavenly peace . . ."

One of the American soldiers joined in in English, belting out the song in a boisterous baritone that got everyone laughing. Mama and Papa started singing, and then the Marzens, until the whole table was joined with song, shaking the roof to its rafters and filling everyone with a warmth that nothing could ever take away.

CHAPTER 28

Boss raised her head and listened. The humans were making noise again, the same sort of noise that Juliette and Antoine had made earlier.

It was foolish, being that loud. It could alert the enemy.

But they'd earned it, especially the pups she'd traveled with. They'd had a long one today.

She rose from her bed of hay in the stables. Around her, her pack members dozed. It had been a stressful day, between getting here, worrying about Tank, watching the others arrive from the forest one by one. But now, the mission was over, at least for a while. They deserved a long, deep sleep.

But there was one packmate missing.

Boss heard the soft bark from the door. Delta stood there, glancing back at Boss. Boss understood the call and followed her.

They leapt together into the night, through the streets of the small town and off into the snowy countryside. As they ran, Boss thought about how wrong she'd been about Delta. The dog might not be as fast or as coordinated as she was, but she was in many ways so strong and so clever. And she'd never backed down—when Tank needed to be dragged along, when Juliette and Buzz needed saving, Delta was always there by her side. No matter their differences, she was, by Boss's standards, a good dog.

Delta stopped, raised her head, and stared off in the distance. Boss looked, listened, smelled deeply . . . and realized what her packmate had sensed.

The enemy soldier, the one who'd stitched up Tank and let the human pups sit by his fire.

He was out there, walking among the trees, breathing heavily. He wasn't heading toward them, but away, deeper into the woods.

The hair on Boss's back rose. Delta growled, letting Boss know she was ready, that at a moment's notice she would run out and take the enemy down.

But no.

Boss woofed and nudged Delta. Not this human. He smelled like the enemy, but he wasn't the enemy. Maybe he wasn't friendly either, but from what Boss had seen, they didn't need to take him out. Not today.

She barked and bounded off up the hill, loving the deep snow as it blew up around her. Delta joined her, and the two ran and leapt and rolled in the snow all along the hillside, chasing each other around as excitedly as though they were on a hike with Gregor. Then they ran as fast as they could back into town, feeling the cold air in their lungs and the night all around them, and knowing that no matter what the world threw their way, they wouldn't have to face it alone.

BATTLE FACTS

The Battle of the Bulge was one of the most important battles of World War II. But what actually happened in this historic chapter in world history?

What was the Battle of the Bulge?
The Battle of the Bulge was a German counter-offensive attack—an attack led to force back an invading army—that occurred from December 16, 1944, to January 16, 1945. It took place in the thick woods of the Ardennes region of Belgium, France, and Luxembourg. The attack was intended to both break through Allied lines in the area as well as keep the Allied forces from reaching the city of Antwerp, which was a major port in Belgium.

The battle took place after German and Allied supply chains into Europe had been cut off, and both armies were beginning to starve. Rations were low, and supplies weren't coming in. Between this and the advance of Allied forces since the invasion of Normandy, German soldiers had begun to lose confidence in their ability to stop the Allies. Many began deserting their posts.

At first, the battle seemed to go to the Nazis, who took advantage of Allied overconfidence and poor reconnaissance (intelligence provided by scouts and spies). This resulted in the Allies sustaining the highest casualties of any operation in World War II. However, the German's weapons and ammunition were also depleted, and they sustained heavy damages to their air force. This allowed the Allies to regroup and reinforce their lines. On top of that, the Nazis were unfamiliar with the snowy and forested terrain of the area, which allowed local defenders to protect their home against Nazi forces.

Eventually, with their weaponry and supplies running out, the Nazis were forced to fall back, and their counteroffensive failed. However, the losses sustained by the Allies made this the single bloodiest battle fought by the United States in World War II, and the second deadliest battle in

US history after the Meuse-Argonne Offensive in World War I.

Why was it called the "Battle of the Bulge"?
The Nazis' strategy in the Ardennes was to attack and eventually push through a weak spot in the American line. The proposed tactic would cause a section of the line to "bulge" out on maps of the battle—hence the name.

BATTLE

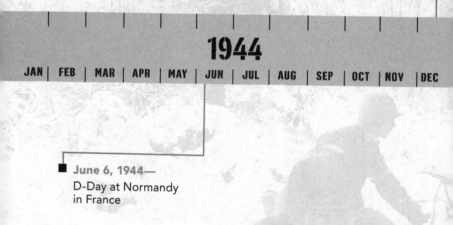

- **December 16, 1944—**
  German counteroffensive begins.

- **December 20, 1944—**
  The Battle of Bastogne, a major standoff between the German and Allied forces in the town of Bastogne, occurs.

- **December 23, 1944—**
  Good weather allows the Allies to bomb German planes and armaments, crippling the Nazi air force.

1944

| JAN | FEB | MAR | APR | MAY | JUN | JUL | AUG | SEP | OCT | NOV | DEC |

- **June 6, 1944—**
  D-Day at Normandy in France

TIMELINE

August 6, 1945—
Atomic bomb dropped
on Hiroshima

August 9, 1945—
Atomic bomb dropped
on Nagasaki

August 14, 1945—
Japanese forces surrender

May 7, 1945—
German forces surrender

May 8, 1945—
V-E Day (Victory in Europe)

1945

| JAN | FEB | MAR | APR | MAY | JUN | JUL | AUG | SEP | OCT | NOV | DEC |

January 1, 1945—
Operation Nordwind, the
Nazis' last major offensive on
the Western Front, occurs. It
is a push for Hitler's troops to
wipe out all Allied soldiers.
However, the exhausted
Germans have severely depleted
their supplies, and the
operation is overall a failure.

January 7, 1945—
His troops beaten down and
his strategy unsuccessful,
Hitler agrees to pull his
soldiers out of the Ardennes.

September 2, 1945—
V-J Day (Victory in Japan),
Japanese sign surrender

WARTIME Q&A

What was rationing like in Occupied Belgium?
Belgium had a rationing system in place in case of occupation, but Germans quickly implemented their own unfair method of regulation. Belgians only received two-thirds of the food that German soldiers did, which was one of the highest differences in rations between soldiers and citizens in Europe.

Belgian citizens were allowed 7.9 oz. of bread (about half a loaf), 8.8 oz. of butter (about two sticks), 2.2 lbs. of sugar, 2.2 lbs. meat, and 33 lbs. of potatoes every month.

Both German soldiers and Belgian citizens were given bread tickets to give to a local baker, but often the baker would either take them all and give everyone an unfair amount, or the Germans would use their power to extort more bread out of the bakers.

On average, Belgian citizens lost fifteen pounds the first year they were occupied.

What is *Graubrot*?
Graubrot is a dark-brown rye bread used by the

German government during World War II. It's not bad when it's made right, but in the huge quantities that bakers were required to make it during World War II, it was not great. It was also tougher and more bitter than the baguettes and white bread that most French and Belgian citizens were used to before being occupied by the Germans.

Were sled dogs actually parachuted into France?
They were, though sources vary about their involvement with the Battle of the Bulge. Over two hundred sled dogs were parachuted into northern France. These dogs were trained at bases in Greenland, Canada, and the northern United States by mushers and trainers who famously "spoke dog" and would train them to be both sled pullers and rescue dogs. Sled dogs were also parachuted into arctic territories in Scandinavia.

When preparing to drop into a hostile territory, the dogs would first be taken on a long hike or run to tire them out. Then they'd be strapped into bucket seats on plane, which was flown at such high altitudes that the air would become thin and difficult to breathe in. The lack of oxygen would put the dogs to sleep. This was done to prevent the (understandably) nervous dogs from fighting or getting upset.

After they landed, the dogs would either pull a sled or would be sent off with supplies. Sometimes they carried food and alcohol to American soldiers out in the field (it was believed that brandy and scotch, alcoholic drinks, would warm the soldiers in the bitter cold, a concept that has been proven to be a myth). Other times, they would carry munitions and other supplies to Allied bases in need.

Different sources have different accounts about how involved sled dogs were with the Battle of the Bulge. Some say that when the idea to drop dogs into France was first suggested, many military leaders thought it was ridiculous. Other sources say it wasn't approved until the snow had already melted. But some claim that famous World War II leader Lieutenant General George S. Patton Jr. thought the plan was genius, and he pushed for American and Canadian dogs to become paratroopers.

BATTLE OF THE BULGE STATS

DATES: December 16, 1944–January 16, 1945

LOCATION: the Ardennes region of Belgium, France, and Luxembourg.

TANKS DEPLOYED: 2,644

GERMAN CASUALTIES: 63,200 to 98,000

AMERICAN CASUALTIES: 89,500

WHAT'S THE SETUP OF A SLED DOG LINE?

Here's how a line of dogs pulling a sled is set up:

Musher   Wheel dogs   Team dogs   Swing dogs   Lead dogs

Lead dogs: These are two dogs at the very front of the line, who lead the way. They have to steer and keep pace, and they must be intelligent "alpha" dogs who know how to find a trail with the best conditions.

Swing dogs: These dogs (like Boss and Buzz!) are second in line, and they have to help steer and navigate around curves in the trail. They have to be smart, coordinated, and loyal.

Team dogs: These are the majority of dogs in a sled line. They have to be powerful so as to help pull the weight of the sled. These are the dogs who do a lot of the hard work for the musher.

Wheel dogs: These are the two dogs closest to the musher. These dogs have to be calm in temperament and able to communicate with the musher and the rest of the pack.

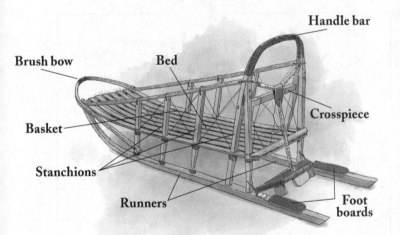

TIPPER

MARINE HERO DOG

NATIONALITY: AMERICAN

BREED: ALASKAN MALAMUTE

STRENGTHS: BRAVERY, LOYALTY, DETERMINATION

TRAINING: CAMP LEJEUNE, THIRD WAR DOG PLATOON

STATIONED: GUADALCANAL, IWO JIMA

HEROIC MOMENT: SPOTTED A CAMOUFLAGED JAPANESE SNIPER IN A TREE, SAVING HIS PLATOON

BEAUTY

SEARCH AND RESCUE
HERO DOG

NATIONALITY: BRITISH

BREED: WIRE-HAIRED TERRIER

STRENGTHS: COMPASSION,
CREATIVITY, DEDICATION

TRAINING: SELF-TAUGHT

STATIONED: LONDON

HEROIC MOMENT: FINDNG OVER 60
BURIED ANIMALS IN ADDITION TO
HUMANS DURING SEARCH AND RESCUE
MISSIONS

HONORS: PDSA PIONEER MEDAL,
DICKIN MEDAL

Join the Fight!

DON'T MISS THE NEXT
ACTION-PACKED MISSION

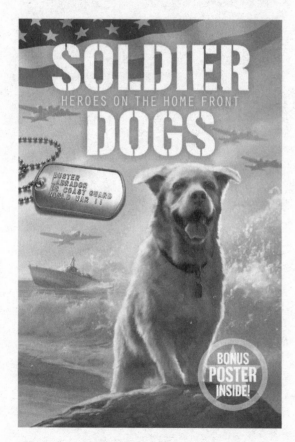

As the riptide pulled him out to sea, Charlie still couldn't believe the war had come to him. Right here, to his hometown.

All around him bobbed pieces of burning wreckage, hunks of wood and metal. Huge slicks of flaming oil blazed along the surface of the water.

He knew about what was happening across the world—the war was inescapable. Every day on the radio, he heard reports of Hitler's march across Europe, through Poland and France, and the bombing on Pearl Harbor. And he saw the struggle at home every day when he walked down the street and never encountered a man between eighteen and twenty-five.

But he'd never dreamed he would die in the war. He was only a kid!

He swam toward the human chain that had formed in the ocean to rescue him. His twin sister, Katie, shrieked his name and reached out to him. But no matter how hard he struggled, he couldn't get to her. Quite the opposite—with every second, the water pulled him farther and farther away. It was like the sea was hungry and wanted Charlie for a snack.

A wave crashed over Charlie's head. Water filled his mouth, and he choked and coughed. He thought of Buster, his faithful dog, who'd been taken away by the Coast Guard for basic training. If only Buster were here now to help him. He couldn't believe the old boy was gone.

As his muscles grew tired, and Charlie found himself unable to keep treading water, he thought again that it made no sense that the war had found him here. In Florida! The war happened in London, and Paris, and Tokyo! Not here! Not America!

Another wave hit him in the face. Charlie sunk below the surface, swallowed by blackness.

Read them all!

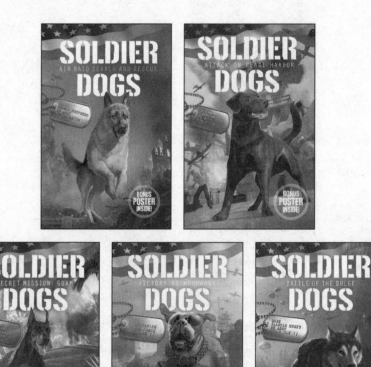

Love dogs?
You may also like...